PEOPLE AND WEATHER

P.J. Kavanagh

JOHN CALDER
London

First published in Great Britain in 1978 by
John Calder (Publishers) Ltd.,
18 Brewer Street, London W1R 4AS

© P.J. Kavanagh 1978

ISBN 0 7145 3666 0 Casebound

ALL RIGHTS RESERVED

No part of this publication may be reproduced, stored in a retrieval system, or transmitted in any form by any means, electronic, mechanical, photocopying, recording or otherwise except for the purposes of review, without the prior written permission of the copyright owner and the publisher.

Any paperback edition of this book whether published simultaneously with, or subsequent to the casebound edition is sold subject to the condition that it shall not, by way of trade, be lent, resold, hired out, or otherwise disposed of, without the publisher's consent, in any form of binding or cover other than that in which it is published.

Photoset in 11/12pt Baskerville by Specialised Offset Services Ltd., Liverpool
Printed by M. & A. Thomson Litho Ltd., East Kilbride
Bound by Hunter & Foulis Ltd., Edinburgh

For Catherine

PEOPLE AND WEATHER

1

It was the time of year when yellow pine-needles lay at the side of the road like damp sand; a brilliant November.

William stopped and glared into the hedge, its roots at his eye-level. A fluffed-out robin hopped about inside it, apparently glad of his company. William climbed into the hedge too, scratching himself on barbed branches, smelling the damp earth-smell. The robin flew off and William took its place, looking upwards through the hedge at the thin blue sky.

A figure walked past in a new gamekeeper's hat, a dark mackintosh and a muffler.

'You've got dirty shoes,' said the Vicar.

'I've been through Owen's farmyard,' replied William, rolling comfortably on his side on the bank-top.

'Sue him,' said the Vicar, who was Welsh, walking on, briefly pausing and touching his hat to a face at a cottage window that vanished as soon as it had spotted him.

William touched his hair and inspected his fingertips. It didn't seem to come off, the stuff from the tin.

He rolled down the bank on purpose, irritated with his body for warning him to fear the slight jolt at the bottom.

It was really too far to walk from his cottage to the bus-stop. Too far for him twice and probably too far for Helen once, as the return journey was mostly uphill. He should have brought the car, uncertain as it was of starting, but then he would not have been able to look at her, concentrating on the road. He was unrepentant, he had walked, although he was weak-legged, light-headed.

At the main road he turned his back on it and held the iron railings of the field by the bus-stop. He looked down at the white scar-tissue of his palms, relic of the old accident, yellowed by the rail. Oxygen eating the iron, cold sun eating him. In the field a chestnut foal was grazing by its grey-flecked mother, he could almost taste its chocolate colour. Turning, he could derive an inky taste from the aluminium sides of the huge container lorries that hurtled past.

He also kept an eye open for the bus. It was apt to forget the scheduled stops between villages. The driver would accelerate past, glazed, as though fearful of ambush. William hopped in the road when he saw it coming, waving his arms. It tried to ignore him but at the last minute slowed down and came to a halt only twenty yards past the sign. There had been time to glimpse Helen inside making greeting gestures and the side of the bus was white with faces turned to see who she had been waving at.

William examined her. Loose green coat, green shoes, unsuitable for walking, loose hair, a calm expression. A big girl: you couldn't put this one in your pocket; or eat her. He kissed her cheek and she hugged him with a sisterly pressure that annoyed him. Pushing up the wide sleeve of her coat he held her warm wrist in one hand and took her hand with the other. Hers was cool and long, like her feet, and he knew how his coolness next to hers must feel papery, knobbed. He held on.

'Edward as gloomy as ever?'

'Is Edward,' she said, inscrutable.

'The children?' 'Fine.'

They started to walk, William telling her it was a long way.

'Good.' She took his arm and squeezed it. '*Lovely* William.'

As they climbed the sun sank, the hedgerows turned black against the sky's orange, a deep black that made the surface of the sunken road appear brighter because of the darkness at its sides. He was glad of her shoes because they gave him the chance to go slowly. It was a steep pull.

'Edward's bringing you down something else to walk in I hope. It's very muddy where we are now.'

'How did you find it?'

'From an Australian in a pub.'

She put a large silk scarf over her head and tied it under her chin, defining her face as though for inspection. William had known her since she was fifteen and she had not changed, only become statelier by imperceptible degrees, although less fat. 'An Australian?'

'They're all over the hills here, conserving away. At night the badgers are like buskers performing for queues of them hidden in bushes. I visited one the other day – he's writing a book about mullion windows or something – and he was very shocked. "Billy," he said, "you just walked on some *speedwell*."'

'You've always lived in such lovely places.'

'Each dingier than the last.'

It was quite dark now and very cold. Ahead of them was one brilliant star. They had been walking for some time, climbing, and she had not asked how much further, or where. A barn owl flapped across the road in front of them, luminous, as though it had a dim light inside it. Helen also seemed to contain light, he could still make out her face in the darkness, whereas he imagined his own to be invisible.

'How's Beryl?' She asked it calmly, cosily, and William was shoved firmly into his domestic situation.

'You make her look like a lamp that's gone out,' he said. 'Like a pain in the arse,' he added, experimentally.

'I think you're both saintly.'

There were more stars now; they cast shadows on the high lane they were walking along. The air was faintly scented as though with the remains of the daylight; the frost which was about to fall had already turned the lock, nothing breathed or sweated. They arrived at a field gate and William touched the cold moisture on the top of it, delaying, making dark marks. Then, with a sigh that sounded like a snort he pushed the gate jerkily over ground, bumpy with the hoof-marks of cattle, and they crossed the field. Around them were the rhythmic, tearing sounds of cattle feeding, shadows moved and stopped munching as they passed; a dark community in the night. They went through another gate into the barnyard, William directing Helen away from the muddier bits. She was incompetent at following his instructions.

On the other side of the yard was the cottage, lightless from the back, and when they moved round to the front, yellow light spilling out of it onto the brick path, Helen stopped and took deep breaths of the smell of hay and cow-muck and cold starlight. 'What a marvellous place!' she said.

William agreed, shortly. It was indeed a good place but in the wrong way. Only a cowman was worthy of it and William was not a cowman but a kind of refugee.

On the other hand the cowman refused to live there.

William regarded the low-level mist that filled the dips in the little valley in front of him, looking at the shapes of the distant trees.

He checked an impulse to go down on his knees on the crisping grass in one of his daily, hourly, attempts to embrace the physical world. He resisted not only because he would wet his trousers but also because, after a round walk of nearly eight hilly miles, he was uncertain whether he would be able to get up.

Meanwhile Helen had gone to the door and half-opened it, calling Beryl with a note of expectation in her voice as though certain her arrival would give pleasure. William heard the pleased answer from inside. He had hoped Beryl would stay where he had left her, in bed.

Instead she was moving vaguely round a table laden with tea things, mugs, a loaf like an old-fashioned hairstyle; she had pushed the table out of its usual place, it was now against the whitewashed wall like a buffet, with a shaded oil lamp on it, making the room look different; pretty, but different, reminding William what a bother it was, after all, to have people to stay.

Beryl and Helen talked comfortably with each other. William sat at the head of the table in the shadow of the lamp wondering if his eyes were glinting, like a bird of prey. He had wanted Helen to himself. Beryl's hair when she moved her head hit the side of her thin face without bouncing, whereas Helen's hair was elastic; if he crumpled up a handful and then let it go, it would burst back to its natural shape, and there was a fuzz of shorter hairs over the surface of it which shone. He would have liked to stand behind her and run his hand gently over those small outstanding hairs, it would have been like touching light.

She was munching her food with relish; they were talking of people they knew. Was the girl quite without malice and shadows? Had she never felt spite? He sat crumbling bread, and thought: 'we are in the presence of an angel'. Angelhood did sometimes descend, in this case into the by no means ethereal body of a girl of twenty-four who liked jokes, men and food, probably in that order. Of course it was nourished on money – that dreadful grandfather – but William did not reduce the scale of her gift on that account. It was what money was for, though we forget it. Besides, he had seen the same gift in cases where money had nothing to do with it. It was a grace that might leave her, or might stay; meanwhile he admired.

The women took the plates from the table and Helen made a parody of shooshing the menfolk out of the kitchen. William knelt to adjust the fire, Beryl had made it up and it smouldered sadly; he cursed the inadequate tongs that for years, and in different houses, he had meant to do something about.

'*Rien ne dure comme le provisoire,*' he muttered; his bones ached, he had difficulty getting up, in fact he didn't get up but fell back half-crouched into a chair that caught him behind the knees. 'Oof.'

'What?' called Beryl, who had been enlivened by the evening.

In the kitchen they were talking about Helen's children. William could summon no interest in them. To him all children were nondescript, and remained so unless he made an effort to get involved with them, and then they became so exhilirating that William could hardly bear it. He looked up at an unframed, curling photograph of his son, a snap leaning on an upper shelf, and cringed.

'Bah!' he said.

'Bah!' said Helen, coming out of the kitchen, drying her hands.

'My old bones ache. I think I walked too far,' said William.

'I think I did too – and half as far as you. Still, I'm glad we walked, it led up to this place beautifully.' She stretched and yawned, behaving like a daughter at home. 'D'you mind if I use your telephone? I ought to let Edward know I've arrived, find out how he's coping.'

William could see her long legs, knees together, jack-knifed sideways on the stairs as she sat murmuring into the receiver behind the half-shut door, making contented um noises as though she and Edward were sharing the same pillow: a recipe for loneliness in the eavesdropper.

Beryl, looking tired now – it had for her been a long

evening – smiled Goodnight to William silently and climbed past Helen on the stairs, lightly touching her head as she passed. Helen said Goodnight without covering the receiver. 'No, that's Beryl going to bed. Yes I will.' She incorporated them all in her hopeful, loving world, Beryl, Edward, William. William did not feel incorporated.

She came back into the room and went to her bag which was hanging on a chair, came across and handed him the money for the call, which he put in his pocket.

She looked down at him uncertainly, then she sat in the chair opposite, on the edge of it. She wanted to go to bed.

'You're very special,' said William, aggressive.

She took it well, grinned, allowed a small silence as her acknowledgement. 'I saw your picture book on trees. It looked lovely.'

Always talk to artists about themselves, her mother must have taught her that. William moved in his chair, and grunted.

'Oh, you never like your own work!'

'I'm a disappointed man.' William smiled, as though to contradict what he said. The effort to be charming, after so long a lapse into direct grumpiness, invigorated him.

'You! Why?'

'Because I've never got down a tenth of what I see.'

'Everyone feels that.'

Damn the girl, who's talking about everyone? 'I don't feel it, I know it.'

William got up to turn down the lamp; they were saving the generator because he'd forgotten to get petrol for it. He wanted to see her face in firelight.

'If you know more than you said, why didn't you say it?'

'*Well*,' said William, teasing, sitting down on the edge of his own chair, his face near hers. 'Well?' she said, turning her face to his. It was William who sat back.

'Because I fell into two pits. The pit of loving my wife and the pit of loving my child.'

'Why pits?'

'You can't see over the edge.'

Her face looked pouchy, lit from beneath by the dying fire. William went on. 'Feelings are inner – the world is outside.'

'Edward sometimes says I have no inner life at all.' She

sounded quite satisfied with the idea.'

'I expect you haven't.'

Her head jerked up. 'Why do you say that?' She was sharp, startling William.

'You don't need it,' he said quickly.

'One can become too dependent,' she said, frowning at the fire.

This was not what he had intended at all, a thoughtful Helen. It was at her apparent absence of thought he'd hoped to warm himself. A philosophizing Helen was not his hearth at all. Now all that was left to him was a grandfatherly cheering up, a metaphorical knocking out of the pipe (he didn't smoke) and a stretching, as for bed. He'd boshed it, like a young man.

Yet there was this splendour sitting in front of him, which had to be acknowledged. That sort of thing was supposed to be his job.

'It's all right to be dependent. Even if you lose people a kind of iron ration is rushed up to the front.'

'Some people crack.'

'What's that to do with you?'

'Edward —'

'Edward's a kind of explorer, tough as an old boot. You're his base-camp, whatever he says.'

'I *like* feelings. I like the feeling I'm feeling. I wish he wouldn't get so savage.'

'With you?'

'With himself.'

'Let him.'

'Yes.'

She still sat forward on the green wooden chair, padded in darker green, in her light green dress; her legs together, sideways, as they had been on the stairs. Whenever William thought of her it was like that, the angle of her long legs, ankles uncrossed; vulnerable and balanced. His boots steamed comfortably on one side of the fire, her long, narrow shoes lay neatly on their sides on the other. He stood up, sensing a hairy expanse of jacket and jersey and thick trousers falling away endlessly from somewhere under his chin. He wondered how he looked. She stood up in her stockings and he was surprised how much shorter she was, shoeless: flat-footed, like a woman expectant in a bedroom. He was uneasy, making too much fuss of the clock, winding it.

The weather had changed, the night had become cloudy outside and a wind tore at the roof, boomed in the chimney. He heard the bed creak upstairs as Beryl got into it.

He didn't want Helen there. She was nothing to do with him. Like the shining foal and the rust on the railings, like the wind outside, reinforced by the lonely mewing sound of an owl – it'd be in that contorted, hopelessly tangled apple tree in the corner of the wall; he'd seen the droppings – she was yet another form he was required to observe, absorb, but only with his eyes, until he could feel his eyes bulge. Eyes, it was always eyes, what about tongue, nose ... She wasn't even a hedge he could crawl inside. He wasn't even allowed to touch.

He put his hands on her shoulders and made what he could of the feel of her bones. He must have held her too long, concentrating, because he felt her totter slightly, losing her balance under the pressure of his hands, which he dropped. Not before he had seen her eyes come to rest briefly on his hairline, before returning, with too much determination, to meet his own. That stuff must show. He was always getting it into the pores of his scalp.

'Come on. I'll show you to the bathroom. You'd better have a candle. I'll get the generator working tomorrow. Your room's on the right at the top of the stairs, I heard Beryl light you a lamp in there, and there's a paraffin heater. Smells a bit.'

Just as well she'd see the bathroom first in shadow, it looked pretty terrible in electric light. Without a damp course there was a curious black fungus that collected on the walls. No use brushing it off, it only came back next day. After taking her through the kitchen, kissing her quickly on the cheek, he returned to the sitting room, banked the fire under its ashes, took the lamp and climbed the stairs, regretting his unbrushed teeth, but he couldn't queue. Tomorrow night he must go first. He heard the plug pull and Helen came out. He stood with the lamp at his own bedroom door lighting her way. 'Good night,' she whispered, waved, and shut her door. He stopped for a moment and considered her undressing. What had he left but his eyes to enjoy her with?

People and Weather

The flame inside the lamp chimney shivered in the draught that came up the stairs, even though the door at the bottom had been shut by Helen – that was thoughtful of her. He sighed, turned and entered his own room.

Beryl, lying on her side, gave a small purr of welcome, something she did whether awake or not, so light was her sleeping. He undressed as quietly as he could and slipped in beside her, grateful for the warmth of her back after the chill of the room. He curled round her and she adjusted herself. They fitted together like two stacked chairs.

As his body warmed he enjoyed the chill of the air on his uncovered cheek. Couldn't stand central heating. No contrast.

A car sighed on the lonely road at the top of the field, changing gear as it approached the bend, the noise fading but becoming clearer as it wound down into the village, as though defined by the surrounding silence, then, at last, becoming a part of it.

He was not who he had thought he would become when he was a boy.

Got the glasses on those small tweeting birds that rise like larks, but in groups. Meadow pipits. On the ground they walk stiff-legged. Distinctive. He stretched his own legs out stiffly and turned on his back, pushing at the tight bedclothes with his toes. They'd done a good job putting him together. The best thing today had been the little group of holly trees on the north slope. Dark green, shining; red berries; the overgrowth of Old Man's Beard, so light grey it was almost pink, and the brown earth under the five small trees tramped pinkish-bare in a circle by huddling sheep. It blew this morning, and bucketed down, from the west. His left cheek had been numb as he'd looked at the holly grove. How long for? Long enough to be soaked to the bone, and pleased with himself. He was hardy. Not bad at sixty-three and made up of bits and pieces. This passion for naming things, for facts – it still grew. It had begun then, after the accident. What a sight he must have been. Beryl had been good. He must have been repulsive. A monster, built up bit by bit, operation after operation. What did that poet say?

I have exchanged formalities with Cerberus
and that's going far enough.

It is. And I did. I began naming things after that. Then, after Peter ... it got worse. Or rather, better. A *passion* for naming things. I love things. Not people. Inhuman? Nonsense. On the contrary. Not sure I'll be able to go on writing those pieces. Can't get people into 'em. It's all things, glorious *things*. More interesting. Who'd have thought it? Edward may be able to do both. The outside and the inside. I wonder. Have hopes for Edward.

Have hopes.

2

It was a bleak, nondescript village, high up for that part of England, with nothing between it and the east wind that blew across Europe from the steppes of Russia. The prevailing wind was westerly, from the distant Atlantic, and by the time it had been forced up a thousand feet it had grown teeth, but not nearly as sharp as the ones that tore at your face and ripped through the high thorn hedges when the wind was in the opposite direction. One way or another there was always a wind up there, even on the calmest day there was a small movement of air tugging your cheek, and the stone angels on the box tombs in the churchyard were appropriately windswept, depicted with their frocks blown sideways, and eastward.

The only remarkable thing about the village was the church, very tiny, but intricately carved with demons, signs of the Zodiac, rats; and even, on the west side, an unexplained Egyptian *ankh*. Nearly everything about it was unexplained; why so undistinguished a village should have so weirdly decorated a church, for a start. And although generations of vicars had done their best to make it dull, blocking up doors, whitewashing wall-paintings (one, startlingly, of *Saturn* – the seventeenth centry vicar had run his knife through that one), moving carvings from their original positions to ones less appropriate, and so on, the church remained an oddly magic place, slightly menacing among the cold gusts of the hilltop. William was by no means certain that all the magic was white.

He was stone-walling at a high point behind his cottage,

looking at the way a flat stone, long fallen, had become green, a darker green than the surrounding winter grass; he tried to shift it with his toe but it was trodden in solid, so he used the point of his pick to lever it up. The earth was naked underneath, crusted with roots of grass like white veins. Helen came round the corner of the cottage to look at the day and watched his distant figure in a dark blue workman's coat holding a stone and looking down at it. The wind, cutting round the cottage corner, made her shiver and clutch her arms across her chest. Arms folded, hunched, she went back to the cottage where she and Beryl, both talkative, were tidying up. She liked the lonely, mildly heroic tasks men set themselves. They were sometimes unduly grave about these but never mind. She did not envy them and found them pleasantly absurd.

William set the stone in position on the wall, weathered side up; underneath it was the colour of cardboard. Over the wall was a bare cornfield with little spikes of green wheat in neat rows. It fell away to the invisible village and at the visible edge of it, the horizon, he watched a burst of starlings go up like smoke.

He waved to Reg who was walking the track between the green spikes with a mattock over his shoulder, each step he took declaring the belief that if he put one foot in front of the other he would get there in the end: in this case, the churchyard. He was on his way to put the finishing touches to Liz Messenger's grave.

Miss Messenger — everyone called her that — had lived in the same house in the village for eighty years, had been born in it. It was the village shop — nowadays selling only a few packets of cigarettes, a few sweets. William had knocked on the door and bought some sweets so that he could look at her and glimpse the inside of her house. She had humorous eyes, an almost gypsy tan and a beard. The sweets were fetched from a stone shelf in a cold stone passage, and what he could see of her sitting room behind was dark brown, stuffed with objects; it looked as though nothing had been added, or had changed its position, since the turn of the century.

She had died three days before. Taken poorly last week, distant cousins had been summoned from the nearby town. All her friends and near relations must have died long ago.

They arrived up her lane in shiny cars and when they climbed out they were odd-shaped, dwarfish, shaggy; their figures had no relation to the sleek machines.

William, wandering at night, glimpsed them through the windows of her cottage, partly obscured by her miraculous, ever-blooming geraniums on the sill. They sat in a circle round the old lady, in silence as far as William could tell. Rumours went round that the doctor wanted her moved to hospital because her house was so cold and her earth closet so far away. She had electricity and electric heaters but she chose not to use them. Beryl made William go to her neighbours with a fan-heater, hoping they could get her to use it, it was at least safe. The neighbours were doubtful, rightly as it turned out. She was moved to hospital against her will and died at once.

What could her neighbours have done? They had lived next to her, off and on, for most of their own lives, tending her bit of garden for her, doing small favours when asked. Only when asked. She was still 'Miss Messenger' to them. They would cheerfully have sat up with her for as many nights as she wished, freezing, but to offer her something she had not asked for – they could not do it. So she died. They were right.

They went in to tidy up next morning, out of respect for her, so that relations would find everything in order. In her bedroom were unopened parcels, Christmas gifts from years back. Small comforts of woollens and the like which hardy Liz Messenger had scorned. Drawers full of oddments, some of them going back a century, a jar full of wire spectacle rims, a pony's harness as it was lifted off the pony thirty, forty years before. William would have given anything to rummage and let the past she had accumulated run through his fingers. Her belongings were a history of the last hundred years.

The relations arrived again one morning in their cars and began the burning. From eight in the morning till after dark the smoke went up, for two days. William could hardly bear it. It filled him with despair; alone of the village he cared about what was being destroyed, or so it seemed, but perhaps it was not so. What was certain was that he could not interfere, not when those who had known her for fifty years dared not. So the relations destroyed the quiet accumulation and kept only what they recognized as useful to them while William and the rest of the village looked on.

William heaved a heavy top-stone in position and called 'Reg Yards.' The retreating figure stopped, turned, and began walking back. 'No!' cried William, climbing with difficulty over the wall to join him on the track half-way.

Reg Yards stood before him, mattock and spade still on his right shoulder, a short square man with thick grey stockings rolled neatly over the tops of enormous wellington boots.

'Sorry to stop you. You digging Miss Messenger's grave?'
'Finishing it.'
'I'm interested. My son's a grave-digger – in America.'
'Is that right?'
'It's an old churchyard – small – how do you know where to dig?'
'You don't. That graveyard has been dug two or three times.'
'You mean you find bones?'
'Yes. Maybe two sets of bones.'
'What do you do with them?'
'Put 'em on one side and put 'em back when I do the filling in.' For the first time his expression changed and expressiveness came into his voice. 'It's all right. They've been there a long time you see.'
'It must be difficult to dig so deep.'
'I have a good iron bar and two steel wedges. That pile of rocks in the churchyard is ones I've punched out. They never went down more than two and a half feet in the old days. When they come out from the town now they don't want to know about rock. I like to go down five and a half, six, if it's what we call a double.' Reg spoke woodenly, with almost hyphenated pauses between his words; brown face, blue eyes, greying black hair fixed firmly back with oil, all set firmly on the base of the enormous boots that turned up bluntly at the toes. Nothing about him moved, except his mouth, and that not much.

'Have you lived here long?'
'I was born here.'
'In the village?'
'No. Ward Hay.'
'Is that a cottage?'

'Yes.'
'Where?'
'Over on High Piece. Slutswell.'
'But there's no cottage there.'
'It was knocked down, wasn't it.'
'Did you mind?'
'I wasn't living there then.'
'Were you sorry to see it go?'
'It wasn't a bad old place.'

These question and answer routines annoyed Beryl. But he was interested so why shouldn't he ask?

'Do you like your job?'
'It's all right.'
'Would you live in a town?'
'I wouldn't be used to a town.'

He and Reg were at ease with each other: he in search of information, Reg Yards politely determined to give none. William steered the talk to the subject of bells, about which Reg knew a great deal and William nothing. There were some minutes of bell-talk from Reg, almost animated now the subject was on solid ground. William understood what he could, it was cold standing there, and at a suitable pause said, 'When's the funeral?' 'Two o'clock.' 'Well, I'll see you there.' 'That's right then,' said Reg, resuming his slow walk, and William, satisfied, went back to his wall.

The accident had left his sense of touch impaired. His hands, like most of his face, head and neck, had been patched together again, very well. He could feel through them, but intermittently. This made him more than usually conscious of the sensation of touch, it was a pleasure to handle the roughness of the stones. He traced the imprint of a fossil shell with the tips of fingers that gave the impression of having more than the usual number of knuckles.

He was glad he had tackled Reg. Beryl found such conversations boring, but he didn't. What was said didn't matter much, or not often. He now had a solider sense of Reg's presence. You can't just nod to a man day after day and at least they hadn't talked about the weather. It wasn't English to ask questions. Well, damn them.

Reg's summer job was to clean the weeds from around the infant trees in some of the conifer plantations that were being planted all over the hills. Soon the place would look like Norway, but that would be after William's time. All day he did it, slashing with a scythe. He started work two hours before William, at eight o'clock, and was still slashing away long after William had knocked off. In autumn it had been Reg harrowing the vast slope at the side of the cottage. The field had been three times mown for hay. In early summer an aeroplane bombed it with nitrogen pellets like sago. A New Zealander with a smashed face did it, landing in the field to refill and refuel before going hedge-hopping again.

As a result the field was crazily fertile.

Three separate cuts of hay they took, with all the impacting effect of the wheels of cutters, tossers, balers. So the farmer had decided to break up the soil of the field properly and Reg was condemned to harrow that forty featureless acres, his tractor trailing cutting discs behind, for eight days. Up the field slowly, down again, then across, from eight until after dark, when he did it by the tractor's headlights. For eight days his world was the enormous blank field, for ten hours at a stretch – or rather it was the cold and deafening cabin of his tractor, his body twisted so that he could look in front and behind. *Eight days*. Alone.

In a factory at least he would have had companions. To do such work, to 'like living here', he would have to have the patient stolidity of a horse. Perhaps he had. But he was not a horse. William paused with a stone in his hands, his eyes on the hazel hedge; a flight of finches had suddenly left it, leaving a solitary bird at the top, bright yellow, like a decoration. Perhaps of all human qualities stolidity was the most valuable, and the one he would most like to learn.

He began to laugh at the thought of Peter. It was true he was a grave-digger. In Atlantic City.

Nothing so funny in that, of course. Though Atlantic City was a poetic touch. He seemed to want nothing more. Apparently the graves were dug by machine. Peter had always liked machines.

Why should he want more? Peter had removed himself neatly from the middle-class which was clever of him because it is not easy. He had taken up his mild bespectacled position at the end, as it were, of the road. He did something useful and competed with no one. Excellent. William enjoyed for a moment the perfection of his son's choice.

But he had to be careful. At any moment a memory of Peter as a child could weaken him. He leaned on the wall smelling elder shoots he had crushed with his boots as he built.

His passion for Peter, for an object he was always bound to lose, had interested him. It had brought him here, to this wall.

For, as the boy needed less and less of him, his own concentration had been forced outwards. Not towards people because love cannot generalize itself in that way.

The love the martyred Jesuits felt for the North American Indians was not a generalized love of the men who burnt them, but a love of God. In fact it was only possible to care for men, that appalling crew, indirectly by being more interested in what was extra-man; in William's case the world and weather outside their heads and outside his own.

The sun was at its highest point now, not very far above the horizon, it was time he went in to eat and change into less muddy trousers for the funeral. He had noticed without much interest that of late he was becoming dirtier. He relinquished his stones with a sigh, and the wideness of the space around him. He did not much wish to go and join the women.

There were perhaps fifteen people in the church, shut in small wooden pews with doors. An enormous vicar with the Victorian quiff welcomed him and he chose a place at the back. Everyone else had done the same, the first eight rows were empty, the last three were packed. The local farmer was there, owner of the village and Liz Messenger's cottage. The postman (whom William suspected of having run over his cat), the neighbours who had looked after her and one or two elderly people William did not recognize. It was bitterly cold. The Vicar deposited a huge black cloak next to him, apologizing, muttering how much colder it was going to be outside. Reg Yards was stationed by the door, still in his digging clothes but neat as ever. There was a noise outside and he sprang at the door to open it. Four aged undertakers led by a red-haired younger man with a carefully mild expression came into the church with the small coffin, carried it up the short aisle and put it down in

People and Weather

the sanctuary. It was followed by the nieces and nephews, each smaller and shaggier than the last, shuffling their feet in heavy shoes, hands awkwardly in the pockets of enormous black overcoats that bulged in surprising places, as though their bodies underneath had unusual knobs. They and the undertakers filled the front pew on either side, the relations stumbling into theirs, kicking the woodwork, and the undertakers sliding in easily, much practised. William had seen them before, at other local funerals, it was as though they were getting advance value for their own, they were of extreme decrepitude, red-nosed, grey-faced. One had an ingrained brown mark on the shoulder of his black overcoat, badge of his trade, powder from newly-sawn wood. The job of the red-haired man seemed to be the throwing of the carefully prepared handful of earth into the grave.

The service began and they all joined in, led by one of the undertakers who sang with relish in a horrible tenor, lingering on the last syllable after everyone else had finished.

The Vicar, a locum who had not known Liz Messenger and was clearly embarrassed by this, read St Paul, 'Unless a grain of wheat dies' etc. Afterwards in a little sermon he apologized for St Paul going on a bit. He said nothing of the splendour of the passage – or of its unsatisfactoriness, – and nothing of the strangeness of Liz Messenger's life. So uneventful in the ordinary sense, without change or movement, its apparent pointlessness raised interesting religious questions, no, not questions, points. Liz Messenger had carried her life in the cup of herself from birth in her cottage to the grave outside, without spilling or scattering any, had spread herself in no direction, had served in her shop and sat in her window. A nut from Christmas, planted for fun by her neighbour when he was a boy, when she was already well into middle-age, had grown into a walnut tree outside her window until it shadowed her house and was really her only view.

There was poetry in her life which the Vicar did not mention as he spoke, looking cold, of a life now past which he had not entered, the last person not to enter Liz Messenger's life, to be evaded by her. He spoke his few words aware of his coldness, aware of the coldness of the few people in front of him, forsaking the pulpit to be more on a level with them – why? – standing under the curious arches built to lean askew like the angle of Christ's head on the cross, scarcely higher than his head and carefully carved with chevrons in and out, a device to keep out the Evil Eye.

A band of limestone chevrons retreating in, advancing out, like the plans of a fortification, a Maginot Line against incursions from outside, against the powerful presences in the air, ending, decoratively in the centre, almost at face-height, in a face. Of a dragon? A long-snouted beast. William suddenly realized that it was a cunning fox.

Outside, the earthworks surrounding the neat grave were covered with plastic sheeting on which was stuck imitation grass. The Vicar stood at the foot in his long cloak, his face blue, his words lost in the wind and the snarling of a digger that shovelled dung in the farmyard over the wall. The red-haired man stepped forward with his handful of earth, dropped it in, and stepped back.

William walked home, to his wall, because standing out there was the best way, in his opinion, to stay aware of the light. Now the sun was below the horizon the browns and greens had an undercolour of redness which he never would have noticed if he had just stepped out of his door to look. And you had to be doing something, the best kind of receptiveness is always indirect. You can't just stand and gawp, or not for long. You have to be implicated in a landscape, thought William, like old Reg Yards – only not as deep as that, please God!

The trouble was, the closer he approached nature, which wasn't very near, the more he felt a loss of self, a drifting outwards which, although it was what he sought, was something he felt an instinctive need to check. That little tumble of pipits, for instance, which suddenly blew in the wind like a flurry of grey leaves, their movement happened inside him and he was, in a sense at least, their movement. It was as though a dissolving process took place inside him and he had no desire to dissolve whatsoever. On the contrary, he intended for as long as possible to hang on to himself. This is why he was often to be seen, if there had been anyone there to notice, as he noticed himself, grasping the top of a wall and looking outwards, his brown eyes with their orange flecks intent, but his hands, with their patches of white skin making the red of the remaining skin look even redder, holding very firmly on to the rough stones.

It had begun fifty years before in South America. As a boy he had roved all day, sometimes all night, on horseback; he used to enjoy, particularly at night, lying right back on his horse's rump and looking up at the sky. He was thought idle. He was idle. His cheerful Irish father's farm ran down, but William could not have saved it. The family came to England. His father died. It was his last link with South America; an only child, his mother had died when he was three; he sometimes thought he remembered her, especially in dreams, a pleasant visitation.

He had supported himself by writing pieces about the wild-life of the *pampa*. Then, because he enjoyed describing things, he wrote about England with a stranger's intensity, as though he had invented it. His books were direct, unsentimental, about old country ways. They owed much to his own implacable presence. He parked himself on someone who lived locally and waited until he heard something interesting, then he wrote it down. He was helped to do this by his ignorance of the English social system.

The books had a small vogue, he was taken up. He enjoyed it, being vain, and it gave him two enduring friendships. Then the war came and he had had his accident. That rattling about on the ground in a simulation aeroplane, it had gone mad with him inside it, knocked him into pieces, burnt him. He had married shortly before and what a mess he had presented to Beryl. She had been very good about it. Busy with her own career at the time. Oddly, among all the wreckage, as soon as he could manage to get about at all he found the sexual part of him still functioned, he was happy about that. Still, he hadn't been much of a man for Beryl, not for years, in and out of hospital for bone grafts, skin grafts; amazing, what they did.

Some idiots who get the nature bug – and hadn't he suffered enough from them! – think themselves entitled to deride reason, and science. Reason, other men's reasoning, had saved him. Reason was the best thing we had. The bush had its reasons, the birds in the bush had their reasons, the bush had been put there for a reason in the first place. Unless it was scrub and then reason said – Clear it.

And yet —

He couldn't write those pieces any more. The magazines that had been eager to print them no longer existed. Nor did the parts of the country he had walked through, or bicycled through, and most likely, none of the people he had talked to.

But that was not why he could not write them. It was more that he felt disinclined to send back reports from a territory he no longer understood. He had always known there was much he did not understand, of course, but now that was the only thing that interested him.

He did not mind the world having changed. He liked change the way he liked the wind, it reminded him he had a face, existed. But he felt himself changing, and he wanted time to watch that change.

It was as though his feeling for Beryl which had unfolded into his feeling for Peter, which was surprisingly less selfish, was now opened out into an area of the utmost inscrutability, an intimation of self-loss which scared him very much because it seemed to approach the witless.

He was determined to explore but he was also determined to hang on. He was as bad-tempered and unregenerate as ever but for some time now, some years maybe, his head had begun to fill at certain moments with intricate wordless prayers. He strained to hear their formulation but could not catch it. They nearly always subsided as soon as he entered any house, including his own.

3

Helen believed that Edward considered William to be a great man.

Thus it amused and pleased her that Beryl, in common with the wives and womenfolk of other 'great men' who had visited her mother's house when she was a girl, writers mostly, and painters, regarded him with the usual mixture of automatic, half-forgotten affection and conscious impatience. William, most of the time, bored Beryl, she felt.

Nor did she seem to think highly of his work.

'What work? He never seems to do any. No, I know what you mean. Well, it's all right darling. It never seems to me quite as good as it could be. I think he's better than he writes. It'd be awful if he were worse, wouldn't it. I mean, when I don't like the *writing* all that much?'

Beryl was sitting at the kitchen table, *The Times* spread in front of her, unopened, and she stared at Helen when Helen turned round from the sink until Helen giggled. Then Beryl let her own laugh out, rather a barking one, as though she had been holding it back, testing Helen.

'Have you seen our bedroom? You must come up. It's dismal. It's like a Victorian slavey's. A bed, a table, a couple of chairs. There's only a bit of carpet because I *must* have that. When I think what my bedroom was like when I first met William. A little brocade canopy in swags at the bedhead, dull gold; dressing-table, an enormous ottoman thing with an arm along one side – you know? – in canary yellow.'

'William disapproved?'

'Oh no.' Beryl sounded surprised at the question. 'He just looked absurd there. I tried to make our bedrooms the way I liked them – Helen, we've lived in *dozens* of places! It just fell away bit by bit. I don't think William noticed. I'm not sure I did.' Beryl paused, as though wondering. 'William's had a big effect. I suppose anyone does if you live with them for thirty-odd years. Do let me dry.'

'No, I like pottering.'

Helen was washing up in yellow gloves. In front of her, over the sink, was a window onto a bank which looked rather ratty. Ducking slightly she could just see the sky through a fringe of leafless elders, straggly, that grew along the top of it. The sky looked uninviting. 'He loves the open air,' she said.

'A fiend for it. More and more. He goes out to it as though to an assignation.' Beryl laughed again and smoothed *The Times* on the table. Though her back was to her, Helen knew that Beryl wanted to go on talking. In fact a conversation to a back which occasionally turned into a face, with due warning, was Beryl's idea of a good audience. It gave her time to compose her expression, and more time during which she needn't bother about her expression at all.

'Do you miss your profession?' said Helen.

'Oh my dear that was a *very* long time ago. How sweet of you to ask. Well, in a way. It's more an idea than a profession, isn't it. I mean all that showing off, being the centre of attention, friends … Of course I miss it.'

'But the work itself?'

'I gave it up because I couldn't do it. Couldn't sing any more. Not well enough. But you're right, that was the most important part. Rehearsing, getting it right. William loves detail too. He was first attracted to me because of my voice. It reminded him of a bird. He's always preferred birds to people' she added, in a vague fashion. 'Then my voice started to go, then he had his accident.'

'That must have been awful!'

'The accident?'

'Well – both.'

'He looked absolutely ridiculous! Like a mummy. And he used to get so *angry*. That's how I knew it was going to be all right, he got so furious with himself and everyone.'

'Shall I make some coffee?'

'Oh *do*. It's only Nescaff I'm afraid.'

That's what everyone always said – It's only Nescaff I'm afraid. Or else they made a fuss, like an alchemical experiment, with percolators and pipettes and things that looked horribly breakable. Helen broke things a lot and at home drank tea. But this had seemed a coffee-ish sort of house. Still, it was the first ordinary, automatic-sounding thing that Beryl had said and Helen hoped she was not going to become formal and housewifely the way most women of her age did. She opened a cupboard and was relieved to see stout unfragile mugs. 'Why do *we* always have to make the beds!' she said suddenly, reaching up into the cupboard.

'Because men build the walls I suppose,' replied Beryl, surprisingly quickly. 'But we don't anyway. William's always been fairly good about that sort of thing. I'm sure Edward is. Though I do get livid the way William expects to be fed. Why can't he feed himself? He has to sometimes, when this arthritis thing gets me, and then he mutters to himself about what isn't in the cupboard and so on. It's our fault of course. I mean the way mothers bring up their sons to expect it.' Beryl laughed. 'Not that I brought up Peter like that. His meals were perfectly filthy. His wife isn't going to be infuriated by being compared to his dear old Mum.'

'What's she like?'

'I've never met her.'

'That must be rather sad.'

'Why?' ...

'Well ...'

'Don't look so troubled. Do I sound dreadfully unnatural? Of course I adore old Peter, but wives, and kiddies? No, honestly no. Not for me.' Beryl smoothed out the paper again and then slapped it impatiently. 'Why *shouldn't* we make the beds! We're frightfully lazy. We don't want to do anything. Yet we're as tough as blazes. Just watching Peter growing up nearly killed William. He went broody. I loved Peter – I felt I had hardly any choice – but William *liked* him. It was much worse for William when everything changed. He lost his best friend. He knew he would eventually of course, it wasn't possessiveness. But that didn't make it easier. Men have a rotten time you know. They're not tied to the world. At a ridiculously early age they have to decide what they're "going to be". Can you imagine anything more wearing? Then they've the rest of their lives to worry about whether they shouldn't have been something else. Then there's wives, suggesting that the life given them isn't the one they expected – which it probably isn't, stupid cows! Any more than his life is the one he expected. But he's made to feel it's his fault.'

'But you chose, yourself. To be a singer. You worked hard at it, you said so.' Helen brought the mugs over to the table.

'Women choose to be engine drivers and chartered accountants. Fine. We're not still condemned to the spinning wheel, or the spinet. But we still don't have that awful necessity to justify ourselves. Not as women. As women we're self-justifying.' Beryl yawned. 'Or most of us think we are.'

Helen looked thoughtful. '*I* feel sorry for men.'

Beryl looked at her, amused. 'We're a couple of witches.'

Looking over her mug at Beryl, Helen acknowledged how handsome she still was, parchment skin, long nose, delicate eyebrows over rather sharp brown eyes. William's public impatience with her behind her back, and in front of it, could not disguise how connected he was with her. It was always clear that he still valued her good opinion above others.

'Do you prefer men to women?'

'Yes,' said Helen.

'White witches,' said Beryl.

'What's that bell?'

'There's a funeral this afternoon. The local shopkeeper.'

The bell went on in slow, single strokes. They were silent for a moment and then Beryl said: 'The church isn't far away, you can't see it because of the hill ... If William went first I shouldn't mind.'

'Died!'

'That's right. I shouldn't mind. Because I've made a discovery. I don't think, after a bit, that I'd miss him. I'm glad you look more interested than shocked. You really are sweet. It's fascinating. At least to me. I mean – or rather I *don't* mean that I don't love him – or whatever it is. I mean I find I've come to a time when such questions are impossible to ask because they have no meaning. They're simply the wrong questions. When you've lived a bit you can't get at the truth of such feelings without unpicking so much knitting there'd be none left, only wool. And it's really rather nice, to realize that. Of course I'd have regrets. Don't you loathe people who say they've no regrets? How could they *not* have! This life ...' she waved her hand in the general direction of the window, and spoke quite cheerfully, 'is dreadful. We hardly know a soul. Or at least, William seems to know people, God knows how – he exchanges hearty monosyllables with them from time to time and that seems to suffice him – but there's no coming and going, no bustle. All these cottages ... We've lived in a series of desert islands, with William tramping from one side of the beach to the other, peering vaguely at the sea. Not much fun for Woman Friday bent over the cooking pot. I haven't *met* anyone for years, which is why I'm rattling on. I've gone slightly potty. So I think has William. I'm shrivelled up inside like an old nut. And I've come to *like* it. It was the life William wished on me. It suits him. At least he thinks it suits him. But it's an inhuman life. It's made me, probably, inhuman, but I like it. Am I being depressing?'

'I'm not sure ... I suppose most people have grandchildren ...'

'You see? That's my choice, isn't it? I can't blame it on anybody. I *like* my life in an odd way. And I'm not downscrambling your youngness and all that, your lovely babies and Edward. Those sorts of feelings are not an illusion you grow out of, oh no. I'm being rather cheery really. What I mean is that what one chooses – even if one doesn't know one is choosing it at the time – is right. When I married William I didn't know we were going to move round a series of isolated houses, each one a little more dismal than the last – and do not much else. But that's what we've done. And perhaps I did know – without knowing I knew. But it's all right. Things just fall away. Not because they weren't true at the time but because we change. Of course you know that. But you can't know that it's not nearly so bad being oldish as it seems when you're youngish ... Though it's true one occasionally wonders where it's all gone.'

Helen collected the mugs and took them to the sink. The wind was pasting rain against the window so hard it flattened out in horizontal lines that chased each other in parallels down the panes. She shivered. She would not like to end her days in this house. She was still at the stage, she thought, of looking forward to treats, as though still at school. Beryl had talked a lot and Helen felt it was her turn but realized how little really she had to say.

She was prevented from having to try by Beryl saying, 'Oh come on, let's light a fire in the sitting-room, it's such a beastly day' and by the slight noise of William coming in. He almost slunk in, dripping, as though he regretted having to. There were no loud stampings, blowing on fingers, exclamations about the weather outside, suggestions that real life was here, inside the house. On the contrary, he brought the outside in with him as though passing briefly through a shed, in the front and out the back. At the door however, he took off his boots and Helen saw his thick grey socks, the soles pressed to the consistency of felt. She wondered if she was going to smell his feet and realized how physically unattractive she found him. He always appeared so muffled in clothes and although he looked clean he didn't seem to wash much. His nails were dirty and he had not followed her to the bathroom last night. He looked clean partly because of the paleness of his face with its new skin which in fact made him look rather handsome. It was dead in texture and made his eyes unusually lively and bright. And his black hair was neat, brushed across like a wig, perhaps concealing a scar. A little trickle of the black stuff he used to darken it was rolling down at the side of his ear. Helen felt ashamed to notice this but could not understand why he bothered. He said he had to change his trousers to go to the funeral and padded quietly upstairs. Beryl called out to him that there was a baked potato in the oven if he wanted it and he did not reply. Later, as they were lighting the fire, Helen heard him moving around in the kitchen so perhaps he had found it. He left as quietly as he had come in. She felt the weight of being in somebody else's house and of not understanding too much. It seemed almost as if Beryl and William were avoiding each other, but perhaps it was normal. Nor was she sure what was expected of her. She longed for the evening when Edward would come and hoped Beryl would not feel inclined to continue their rather high-level chat now the fire was lit.

She need not have worried. Beryl looked pale, said she was going upstairs to rest. 'I really lead the laziest life. I could stay in bed all day, reading and dozing, couldn't you?'

Helen thought, with a touch of smugness, how long it was, mother of two, since she had had a chance to do that. But she remembered how often she had longed to. 'Oh *yes*.'

'Will you be all right?'

'I think I'll just sit here for a bit, if that's O.K?'

'You do exactly what you want. I won't emerge for ages, and I shouldn't think William'll be in again before dark.'

'I might even work up enough energy to go for a walk. I haven't really seen this place yet.'

Beryl told her where macs and boots were, directions to walk in, counselled her to stay where she was, and went upstairs.

It was very quiet in the house when she had gone. Helen, alone in the small, long room with its red brick fireplace and its low window, squatted down to look at the books that lined the room up to waist-level. She had to move the armchairs to get at some of the them and felt she was prying. Battered ornithological books, books on archaeology, geology, natural history, unexpected books on cars and mechanical engineering she guessed to be Peter's, a collection of W.H. Hudson, some Richard Jefferies, Meredith, Tennyson, Kingsley Amis. On top of the bookcase were ornaments, or at any rate, objects: a bolas with leather thongs, a small gourd ornamented in silver, an ammonite, a Mexican donkey in painted terracotta. In a far corner were some head-level shelves mostly filled with tall art books but there were two or three collections of theatrical memoirs. Helen took down *The Dancing Days*, hoping to find some mention of Beryl. Next to it was a curled photograph of a child about six standing in a field wearing wellingtons, grinning at the camera with that odd pathos children always have in snaps.

She took the theatrical book to a chair and sat down. Sure enough, there was Beryl in a photograph; a scene from *The Night is Young*; bobbed hair, dark mouth, standing, arms linked in a line of other period faces, Beryl in the centre and the rest of the line men, with flat shiny hair and huge jaws like pictures she had seen of Jack Hulbert. Beryl leant back side-on, supported, her face to the audience and one knee raised so that her pleated skirt made an arc. She was wearing pointed shoes, with a strap.

Helen felt oppressed. The crackle of the small fire sounded self-preoccupied and the picture, taken so long ago, was depressing in its ignorance of the future: a gay flirtatious Beryl who now lived in a rain-swept cottage, unwell, with too little to do and no adorers.

While she was thinking this she realized the wind had dropped and so had the rain noise. She turned round and saw a blue, washed sky with fast white clouds above William's bean-sticks which still had twisted brown stalks climbing up them that shook, but not violently, in the breeze. Turned round like that she had her back to the blind wall and there was a loud scratching noise that made her turn round, startled. She jumped, made an exclamation, because she was being watched. Hidden among the books on the upper shelves was a small window, a sort of spy-hole to the north which she had not noticed, so little light came through it. Pressing its nose against it was a flat round face with huge eyes which she took at first to be an owl. There was something wrong about its mouth, a thick string dangled down one side of it and then she realized it was a long-haired cat, black and white with ginger fur around its neck giving the impression of a flat face, and in its mouth was a rat.

It stared at her for a moment, unblinking, then it pushed the window delicately with a white paw, opened it, and jumped into the room. It came towards her and lay down at her feet, looking up. Then it nodded its head, opened its jaws and the rat which Helen, too startled to move, had assumed to be dead, jumped out with a high scream and scuttled to the fender, where it huddled at bay, its fur clotted with wet from the cat's mouth. The cat approached slowly and it let out another scream and hissed from the back of its open throat, so that even the cat seemed disconcerted. Helen, badly shaken, wished helplessly for someone to come in and help her. It was the screaming that frightened her most. She decided the best thing to do was to try and kill the rat so she took the grate shovel and slowly approached it. As it felt her shadow it screamed again and she brought the shovel down with a clatter, missing it by a foot, and it scuttled further, trying to jump up the wall, showing itself to be a small rat, perhaps a young one, with a clean white belly and pink feet, but surprisingly long and with a startlingly elastic jump. Remembering tales of cornered rats jumping at people and biting them, she retreated to her chair and curled her legs up under her. The cat seemed content to take the rest of the day over the game and the rat seemed capable of screaming itself out of trouble. Perhaps if she opened the door it would run out? Apart from disliking the idea of turning a rat loose on the rest of the household she felt she had used up her courage attempting to hit it with the shovel and was unable to move. It made a run for it behind the far armchair and there was a cracking noise; no more screams, only more cracking. After a while the cat emerged and began washing its paws. Helen, feeling sick, went to look. Nothing there, save a neat bag she took to be the spleen or the stomach and the hairless tail. The rat was now inside the cat. She took the shovel, kicked the remains on to it and threw them on the fire.

She went into the porch and put on the red boots and a

coat of shining red plastic belonging to Beryl. Outside it was brilliant. Drops of rain still hung on bare bushes as bright as electric light bulbs in the sun. She took out her shoe and wiped it on the wet grass, threw it back into the hall, shut the door, huddled the coat round herself and went out of the garden gate into the soggy field. A crowd of big black birds was spiralling up and down at the bottom of the green slope and she wondered if there was something dead there too. She did not want the world covered in rats but execution usually took place out of sight. 'Not a sparrow falls, but God our Father in Heaven...'; she had always taken comfort in that but it was impossible to believe that God cared for the rat and therefore extremely difficult to believe he cared for her. When she reached the top of the field she saw the church tower among the trees and suddenly understood, for the first time, the savage insistence of the men who had built it. Six hundred, seven hundred years ago they were surrounded by danger and fear and dark; it wasn't faith that built churches like that in lost places, in wind and mud, it was defiance. It was man fulfilling his nature as inexorably as the cat. 'Look!' he said to the world, to the theatre of constant murder she was walking through, 'we can build higher and taller than you! damn you!' Not 'bless you' as she had thought. For a moment she exulted in her own human power to defy. She wondered for the first time if this was how William felt, with his passion for the Great Outdoors. And she had thought he'd gone out to praise and bless and be ennobled in some vague way. She had thought she admired him for that but, she now realized, without much interest that in her admiration – in Beryl's? it would explain much – there was a drop of female contempt. But it wasn't like that at all. The men who had built that church had been fierce inside themselves, outwardly sullen, not to be overthrown, and William wanted to be like them. Wasn't that it?

Walking on through a gate she found the road and continued a little way towards the church before turning back. There was an untrimmed hedge along the side of the road and a small crowd of birds with black heads and long tails hopped from bush to bush beside her as she walked; they seemed quite tame, preoccupied in their search for food and she became fond of their company. The bell had stopped in the church tower now, so presumably that poor woman was in her grave. She stopped and listened and heard a chink of what might have been a spade on stone, and the noise of a farm engine. Her life was very small — there was only Edward and Sarah and Timothy and the preoccupations they daily brought her. She thought of the future with a spurt of dread that went as quickly as it had come. Again she suddenly felt that sense of exultation, when an instinct told her, very firmly, that the future was none of her business.

She sat for a moment on a broken piece of walling at the roadside and looked at straight lines of green which were just appearing in a wide field. Because of some trick of light she noticed the field was not flat. Running across the lines of green, at an angle to them, were widely spaced lines that were in the ground itself, making long strips. The field looked like a piece of brown paper which had been symmetrically folded and then smoothed out again. She was pleased she had noticed that, she could almost feel in the palms of her hands the soft green prickles and then the slight depression or rise in the lines that marked the old folds, as though she had run her hands over the smooth field.

When she next came to herself she realized she had been thinking of a film she had slipped away to see with Veronica, leaving the children with Veronica's girl. The deliciousness of going to see a silly film in the afternoon and laughing with Veronica! She laughed now, as she discovered she'd been going through the plot, which hadn't been worth remembering. She got up and turned back to the cottage, her head huddled into her shoulders. In all other ways she walked upright, rather boldly, and it was this slight huddlement of her head which deprived her figure of the arrogant, head-thrown-back confidence that belongs to some of the young which some elderly observers, William for instance, found so depressing. It immediately made him wonder when the blow was coming that would change it, or more likely the succession of small blows that would bend the neck, withdraw the chin, depress the head, so that the figure would become, from a hundred yards away, unmistakeably that of someone over thirty-five.

With Helen, however, it was different. She gave the

impression of being at least partially prepared, so an observer, admiring her youth, was permitted to wonder whether it mightn't be just possible, given a bit of luck, that she would get away with it.

4

There was an observer – there always is in hilly places – and it was William. He could hardly miss that figure, bright as a red sweet among all the duns and greys. She looked very solitary inside that crisp shininess. He carefully stood still watching her and then she disappeared and he went back, sighing, to fiddle with a small spring that sprouted out of a collapsed wall in a dip, more or less hidden at the side of the field. He was trying to make it run properly, directing it into a channel which he grubbed out with a spade. He was also trying to trace its source. He drank some of it, wondering briefly about cess-pits further up towards the village. It was, truly, a most undistinguished spot: a collapsed wall, a trickle of water, the whole area spiked with the brown stalks of last year's nettles. It was his by right of his interest in it, he was content there because he could think of no reason why anyone should want to take it away from him. 'Silly old bugger' he said aloud to himself, and there was a laugh behind him. He turned round and there was Edward. It was the noise of the water and the rustle of his clothing which had prevented him from hearing Edward's approach, he assured himself, he did not like to think he could be stalked.

Edward laughed again at his startled face and ran his fingers through his hair; his right hand, moving left to right, a curious roundabout gesture so well known to William that he laughed in his turn and they moved to shake hands each tapping the other with his free arm, pleased.

'I love it. Just playing with water and mud.'

'You've made a sort of arbour here,' said Edward, looking at the half-buried rocks William had set in the bank to sit on. 'Won't the cows muck it up when they come to drink?' he said, sitting on one of the stones, sticking his legs out in front of him, leaning back on the bank. 'Probably,' said William, noticing he fitted into the place in his mud-coloured clothes.

'It's out of the wind too,' Edward said. 'It's like a razor coming down and here it suddenly stops.'

'And out of the traffic noise.' William paused to listen. The wind gusted over their heads through the hedge. He welcomed windy days; on still, quiet ones you could hear the lorries changing gear a mile away. 'You couldn't hear any traffic two months ago. Then they raised the road so the traffic could go faster and chopped down the beeches alongside. One day we could hear the postman's van on its way to us, next it was at the door unheard, lost in the general roar. Does it bother you?'

Edward did not answer, just watched William with eyes that looked small in his long face.

William knew he sounded petulant, but the change, for him, had been a source of fear. For years now he had felt his explorations threatened by a tightening circle of bulldozers. Sometimes they were necessary but as often they were not, and he could see no future for a world which contained only the human. He could certainly see no future for himself. He knew he approached fanaticism on the matter, as well as fogeydom. Rise above – accept. But how could you rise above a foam of tarmacadam and if you did, when you wanted to rest, where would there be to perch? He always seemed to take up a reactionary position the minute he met Edward. Damn. He had not wished to begin by complaining.

'How's the farm?' he said.

'We've planted ten more hectares of vines.'

'Will you be able to cultivate them?'

'If we get the grant we will. Franco will help me on a mezzo-mezzo basis. We ought to be able to produce 750 quintale more a year. About six thousand quids' worth.' He grinned.

'What's your production at the moment?'

'Two hundred quintale.'

William suppressed a gasp. Within seconds of meeting Edward he was already trying to prevent him from recognizing his own absurdity. But he was too intrigued at the size of this latest nonsense to let go of it at once. 'Of your production now do you have any over to sell?'

People and Weather

'God no! We drink it.'
'So you quadruple production – just like that.'
'Marco has.'
'He has about twenty workers, money. You've nobody.'
'It'll mean work of course.'
'Of course,' said William.

They both stared at the little trickle of water emerging from between two heavily mossed stones. Its persistence was like the ticking of a clock, but more varied. William saw Edward in the high dark kitchen of his farm in Italy, long damp logs spitting in the enormous fireplace, Edward staring out of the small window at the overgrown hillside, drinking endless cups of coffee.

It was not that he was lazy. He was capable of working ten hours at a stretch, hacking, pruning, ploughing. It was just that he loved disaster. There was a vein of subterranean humour in Edward and William had never been able to decide to what extent his personal chaos was a joke he insisted that life play upon him; which was, in turn, his comment on life. There was something monumental in it. All the small details of living that worried everyone else, the bare larder, the blocked lavatory, the absence of fuel – all these things Edward made a point of never worrying about at all, so that he could stand in the dark kitchen supperless, as the last lamp flickered, the volcanic eruptions of his lavatory floating round his ankles. Perhaps that was why he always wore boots? Life once more behaving as he expected it to. His triumph was complete. He made William feel mediocre. These things were not, after all, worth fussing over. Edward survived; more free, more young, less burdened than he had any right to be.

The best way to bring about his favourite situation, which was failure, was to think up impossible schemes. His enormously enlarged vineyard was a masterstroke. William, who had been briefly gloomy, felt himself entering into the spirit of the thing and chuckled. Edward laughed too, as though he had been following William's thoughts. 'What time is it?' Neither of them had a watch. The light was going out of the sky and the shoots on the top of the hedge were turned cinnamon colour in the invisible sunset. They climbed the bank towards home and saw the sunset, a thin band of clear yellow, and above it in a straight line a lid of dark evening cloud.

William was tired. He had been all day in the open and these days that made him feel sleepy the moment he got indoors. He did not want that to happen tonight but he had to keep awake somehow: 'It'll be opening time soon,' he said, 'let's go to the pub.'

'Fine,' said Edward. Then he added, to William's annoyance, 'I'll see what Helen thinks.'

William had not asked him or Helen what had brought them to England. He was now too captivated by his vision of those vines turned to bramble-like straggles, in the same condition as the old ones, grapes growing on the ground. He would like to go and visit Edward in Italy. He would suggest it later. The field went suck-suck under their feet as they crossed it.

He disliked female bustle and equally disliked the hush of the house when he returned to it. Beryl was usually preoccupied, reading, or in bed asleep, or sometimes, and this disturbed him, just sitting. She never seemed to be moving about. Helen, however, had somehow managed to turn the cottage into a pleasantly undemanding hive. She was singing in the kitchen, clattering unassertively, there was in the air a distinct promise of evening being welcomed in, of a stage being set, even of food. How *did* she put up with Edward, thought William. He, meanwhile, had gone into the kitchen and was hugging her probably. William heard Helen say 'Oh, lovely' and guessed she had agreed to come to the pub, which meant the postponement of supper to his regret. He wouldn't be able to talk to Edward in the pub anyway because it was sure to be fairly crowded. He took off his boots in the hall and climbed the stairs, hearing Beryl's voice in the kitchen, young-sounding. She liked having people to stay. He took off his trousers, wet from the splashing of the stream, and sat on the edge of the bed. A wave of fatigue nearly drowned him, his eyes closed. He'd be better in the pub. He shuffled into his funeral trousers in the dark, blinking purposely to help his eyelids stay open. He'd still forgotten to fill the generator. There was not much to choose between himself and Edward.

And he hadn't done any money-making work. Fiddling with streams, building walls, and time had passed. It was as though some sort of god was calling him, not altogether a friendly one either, and he must fiddle at his tasks in the open until the god manifested himself and told him what he wanted. This the god never quite did, though leaving enough hints in the air for William to feel required to continue his vigil. For the most part that was good, out in the open, though he grew tired these days. Somewhere inside his chest, or somewhere behind the back of his neck, he couldn't locate it precisely, or decide whether it was physical or mental, there was a presence, a lump, a dark hard something that boded ill and frightened him, as though he was moving too far from ordinary life and his comeuppance was on its way. Most days he could ignore it, some days it went away altogether and he was filled with a pleasant sense of a path well chosen, and he brimmed with self-approval. But it was never far away, this area of darkness that seemed to be waiting until the appointed time when all he valued would be taken away and he would be shown that anything he had done and thought was in vain.

He sat on the checked counterpane of the bed longing to stretch out and thought of Edward, who drove himself further and further into difficulties. Not a bad way to live. He ran his hand over the bed feeling the raised seams stitched by Beryl twenty, no, more like thirty, years before. He thought of Helen, her biscuity smell, her – distance in time from his old patched bones.

Money was running short, however careful they were. That cash from the film-rights – what an absurdity that had been! It had stood them in good stead. He had even written a screenplay after that. Extraordinary. Peter would have been about five ...

He stood up suddenly in the dark and blood rushed to his head. For a moment he swayed, dizzy, then he carefully began to make his way downstairs. Beryl rushed out of the kitchen laughing and began to come up. Her face was filled with the company of Helen and Edward, and as she raised her eyes to William her expression faltered. It was clear that for a few minutes she had forgotten the sort of person thirty years in his company was supposed to have made her. She still smiled, but her spirits were checked; enough to show.

William saw. There was nothing he could do about it. He came down a step in the narrow passage of the stairs and put his hand on her shoulder and tried to kiss her. She turned her head and he got her cheek. It was a clumsy moment but clumsiness seemed appropriate. The blunt wedge under his heart lurched a bit. He had not meant to make Beryl like this. But there was nothing to be done.

'Dear William,' said Beryl busily, moving past him.

He caught her hand as it trailed behind her. 'You're coming then?'

'Well, I thought I would.' She knew he didn't want her to come. She would cramp his style as he had just cramped hers. He confidently expected to make a fool of himself in the pub.

'Good. Don't be too long.'

'I'll just change my skirt.'

He carried on downstairs in the semi-dark, careful not to kick the telephone. Edward and Helen were quiet in the kitchen. William took the opportunity to do what he usually did when he found himself a vessel of cross-currents and vortices that left him breathless. He went outside and took deep breaths, counting; seven in, seven out. It always worked. Looking out into the night he had a sense of the world as a brush and himself as a short bristle on it not significantly different in size from the grass and the dark trees.

Edward came to join him, smoking a pipe. They stood together looking at the evening.

'Are they nearly ready?'

'I think so,' said Edward. 'Why don't we walk? They could use the car and join us.'

'Good idea,' said William, realizing it was what he had hoped Edward would say; he liked walking with him, and pumping his legs to and fro would polish off what remained of the surging and seething inside him. Edward went in to explain and they set off in the darkness across the field.

They were both men who put women at the centre of their lives, so they were starved for male company and welcomed it from each other.

There was however a little game they had to play out between themselves before they could settle down. William knew, for example, that Edward considered him vain, and liked to pander to what he regarded as this amiable weakness. The nuisance of it was that sometimes William perversely surrendered to the temptation offered him by Edward, of talking about himself, hearing his own idiocy, conscious of Edward's deepening silence and gloomily certain he would soon have to listen to Edward complaining about the world.

Edward began it immediately, saying that he had just been re-reading one of William's books with renewed admiration. But William was not to be drawn. Tonight he cared nothing for his work, wondered how he had ever found the time to shut himself away, when life outside was so continuously interesting.

There was a low moon, its shadowy part visible. Only in that condition, thought William, does it give the sense of being globular, as well as round.

Edward was also looking at it and quoted ' "Well, if the bard was weather wise, who made the grand old ballad of Sir Patrick Spens..." I wonder if that means bad weather.'

'It was always supposed so,' said William. Beryl hated wild weather. It was as though she blamed him for it. In a way she was right. Left to herself she would have lived in London and taken precautions for the weather not to impinge upon her at all.

'*Do* the stars make you feel small?' asked Edward.

'Good lord, no. It's only being inhuman that makes me feel small.'

'All the same,' said Edward, looking up, 'there's an awful lot of them.'

'There's an awful lot of us.'

'I know.' Letting it be understood from the tone of his reply that the number of people, like the number of stars, got him down. 'Don't you think we fuss a lot?'

'What about?'

'Love; our precious souls.'

'Not really. Some of us do. Have you been fussing?'

They walked on in silence, their heels striking the road the loudest sound in the small breeze. Then Edward said: 'Women are very critical.'

William was startled to hear his own thoughts about Beryl echoed so quickly: 'Not Helen, surely!'

'No ... No. It's bloody wet where we are you know. Not much doing in winter. Sometimes I catch her – just staring at me.' He turned to William and laughed.

'So you get up and give her a hug!'

'Is that what you would do?'

'If I was sure I wasn't going to puncture myself on one of Beryl's spikes.'

'Can you ever be sure?'

'No.'

Both men laughed, Edward reflecting that there was sometimes a smugness about William and the latter comfortably recalling how on this very road the day before he had youthfully lusted after Helen.

Roosting pheasants crashed upwards through the bare branches above their heads, big as footballs, disturbed by their passing.

'You're monogamous,' said Edward.

'In a way I suppose,' said William, not much wishing to hear any tale of Edward's playing Helen up, if that was what was coming. He felt a great fondness for the absent Beryl. He looked forward to seeing her in the pub, out of place among the smoke and the heartiness; more, he realized with surprise, than he looked forward to admiring Helen. He was indeed smug at the moment; proud of his capacity for pleasure; he was a bottle filled with interest, his head the cork.

He stopped and thrust his hand through thorns onto the wet surface of the bank. The earth was loose, disturbed by mice and rabbits, and tiny nettles that had survived the autumn stung his fingers. The earth felt soft and then, slowly, cold.

'You know, what makes the whole difference is whether one in any way at all believes in an after-life,' he said, standing still, sucking his fingers, spitting, grit from his fingers feeling large as pebbles between his teeth.

Edward had walked on. Now he stopped and turned, almost invisible in the shadow of the hedge.

'If you were being led out to be shot it would matter wouldn't it? Or for that matter if you were in politics,' William asked.

'You mean you'd care less?'

'The extraordinary thing is how long it's taken me to realize it. That's why I don't write any more. I can't catch it.'

'Well, you should write about it.'

'Oh no I shouldn't. You should never write *about* things. It should come out naturally, almost without you noticing. Artist's conscience you know. Writing isn't propaganda. It's inside me as though I'm a bottle. Pull out the cork and I'd spill all over the place. That's bad writing.'

'That's what I missed in *Wasted Time*.'

'Bad writing?'

'You stopped when I wanted you to go on.'

'You never said you missed anything you bastard. You were just saying how good it was. I can't remember it.'

'Yes you can. Why didn't you push it a bit further?'

'And turn into a priest?'

'Risk making a fool of yourself.'

'I hate button-holers, don't you?'

'Depends.'

'Besides, if I spill it all out I might just become an empty bottle.'

'Is your faith as delicate as that?'

'I've been empty – I could be again.'

'When your faith goes you lose faith in it?'

'That's another odd thing,' said William reflectively. 'I can't, now, ever remember doubting.' He walked towards the figure waiting below him and they continued down the hill.

'You've let England make you genteel.'

William stopped, incredulous: '*Me*?'

Edward took his arm and made him continue walking, relieved to see the lights of the pub at the bottom of the hill, risking a bantering tone. 'You come over here with saddle-sores and pampas grass in your eyebrows and are so bowled over by the *niceness* of England you fall for it. But the whole point of England is that one doesn't say certain things – that's what makes it so comfortable. You've a much bigger continent behind your back than Europe. *You* should say them. I've only got my Celtic glooms. These people only have' – he made a gesture at the parked cars – 'whatever the English have.'

'Quite a lot,' said William. 'It's a flattering picture of me, silhouetted against a vast space. I shall have to think about it.' He pushed open the door of the pub and reeled back: 'Good God!' It was so packed it was almost impossible to get in. 'I've never been here on a Saturday before, usually all you can hear is the ticking of the clock. I expected company but not this. Who *are* all these people!' At first appalled he was almost at once cheery and pushed his way to the bar.

He ordered himself a large whisky which he drank quickly. Edward had half a pint of cloudy cider, sipping it, watching William.

William leaned his back against the crowded bar and surveyed the room. 'It's all a question of having the courage of one's own pottiness you know. You never came to that last place we lived in did you? By a lake.'

'By a where?' shouted Edward over the shoulder of a man who came between them to order at the bar. He wished they could find somewhere to sit if William was feeling expansive, but there was nowhere.

'A lake. There was a dipper, you know, a water ouzel, that used to fly along the lake regularly making a metal, chinking noise. You could always see it, even on dark days because it has a white blob on its chest and you could see the blob flying low, in swoops, like a magic ping-pong ball, and there was always this chinking noise to draw your attention. The point is – I thought it was talking to me. It seemed to come out when I was around. It was as though it contained the soul of someone dead, or had a message for me from such a soul.'

'The old idea.'

'Yes. I dismissed it. Or thought I did. But I never saw that dipper without excitement. I used to go in search of it. Then one day I admitted to myself what I really thought. Why not?'

'No reason. I suppose,' said Edward doubtfully; this was dangerous ground.

'Precisely. Reason. That's what I saw and that's what I felt and my reason did everything to prevent me seeing what I was feeling. My reason was helping me to cheat. You follow me?'

'I follow you as much as the dipper did.'

'It's more than possible my interpretation of connection with it was superstitious foolishness, but my reason tried to tell me I was not connected with it *and I was.*' He emphasized the last three words with three jerks of his head, staring at the floor, his hair flopping. 'Why did my mind want to make me dishonest? We're all dishonest in this way. We all believe in a world of correspondences and coincidences, inklings – yes, we *all* do! – why not admit it?'

'Because we're trying to control ourselves,' shouted Edward above the hubbub.

'I see no signs that we succeed. We're only strict with ourselves in this one area. For the rest we're as happily and disastrously irrational as ever. Microscopes show us that the apparently inert is moving all the time. Primitive people knew it and it made them a bloody sight more respectful.'

'Of each other?'

'Are we respectful?'

Edward, trying another tack, mildly embarrassed, suggested that to imagine birds were anything but birds was a form of self-indulgence.

'Oh it's all self-indulgence. Everything except eating and sleeping. And work. Every thought. Every emotion. Living here. Without being a farmer, like you.' He grinned at Edward who was examining the room.

'Wasn't there a wall over there where the fruit machine is? And the darts board on it?'

'Yes.'

'The place used to be full of Thomas Hardy characters, where have they gone?'

'The cider junkies? Some dead. There's one over there. Come on.' William stuck out his chin, blotchy-faced, and pushed his way through the crowd. Edward behind him muttered, 'So much change, in three or four years. Don't you mind?'

'Even I can't expect the place to be kept as my private park. Evening Charlie.'

'Good evening,' said a formally dressed figure in a frayed suit, a frayed collar and tie and a carefully set greening bowler hat. He sat very erect, talking to no one, one hand on a small webbing haversack by his side from which the necks of six quart bottles stuck out, the other hand resting on the head of his stick.

'How's the back?'

Charlie kept his bloodshot eyes on William and funnelled his lips for a long intake of breath, so long that Edward wondered how he was going to speak at the end of it. But he did, after a shake of his chin towards his left shoulder: 'Pretty bad.'

'Still in your suit of armour?'

'Ah.' Same shake of chin. By way of confirmation, he smote himself with the hand that held the stick and gave out a sound like a hollow wall.

'Have they said what's the matter?'

'Nup.' It came out so short that, taken with the shake of the chin, it could be interpreted as a comment both on hospitals and on life, or as a final release of the previous intake of breath.

'Have you asked them?'

'Nup.'

'When will you get out of plaster?'

Same performance, inhalation, shake of chin, exhalation: 'I couldn't say.'

'Well, keep smiling. Have a drink.'

'Thank you.'

'Incurious chap,' said William, as they moved back to the bar. 'Never heard him say anything else to anybody. I like it.'

'How can you like it! It's cow-like!'

'Perhaps. I like animals.'

'That's the most patronizing thing I ever heard anyone say!'

'Is it? I'm an animal myself, like Charlie. Have another one of those.'

'I'll have a pint!'

'Good. I'll have some more whisky. I could drink a bottle. See that fireplace? No, you can't see the bloody thing for people but there's an old fireplace over there. Used to be a Victorian stove. A syndicate bought this place, did it up, took out the stove and discovered the fireplace. Jolly old. You know what? It looks fake. That's frightening. At least it frightens me. It might as well be fake. Like the Georgian bottle-glass in the window. They put that in last year. Because it's only there for effect. Everything in this pub is only for effect. Except Charlie. As long as anybody can remember he's been coming to this place on the dot of opening time with his bottles, staying till closing time and then leaving with his bottles filled to carry him through to the next opening time. He's a woodman. He sits there, upright, correct, saying nothing, or next to nothing, making companionable noises when pressed; sits there while his cronies die, his high-backed nook is swept away, his dark corner converted to a bright bow-window, wooden tables turning to formica tables, the door appearing in a different place, walls disappearing altogether, plaster scraped off other walls to show stone never meant to be shown, he sits there not saying a word and apparently not minding. Soon they'll stop selling cider because it's not economic. He'll drink something else. He won't complain. He's realized how serious life is. No – believe me. He's realized life is a serious dangerous business and he's narrowed himself, without being at all defeated, into the smallest and least noticeable compass he can. He makes no choices, has no opinions, or none that anyone has heard him utter. He has built a wall of habit, politeness and cider and sits behind it saying, literally, "Ah". You still think I'm being patronizing? I say that man is a serious man! Life is dignified by him, and death too. I wish I could feel the same about some of these.' He jerked his re-filled glass towards the groups that hemmed them in and some of his whisky splashed down his front and on to his shoes. 'They don't know what they want. Charlie does.'

'But if he were educated you'd think he was mad.'

William glanced at Edward. 'I would. That's how we use education – to pretend we're full when we're empty.'

They watched a young man with beautiful hair to his shoulders, in the muddy wellingtons of a farm-worker, shovelling tenpenny pieces into the fruit machine. He seemed to have a large supply, and not to mind losing them.

'I thought they were supposed to be underpaid,' said Edward.

'They are,' said William, frowning at the floor. Then, with one of the quick spurts of anger that Edward remembered of old. 'Perhaps he should be spending it on paperbacks by Herman Hesse?'

'It seems a waste of money.'

'It is.'

Somebody behind said 'You meet such fascinating types here' and Edward turned to see who had spoken. He couldn't tell, from among the group standing behind them, which self-consciously fell silent when he turned, and examining a rural England he had not seen for four years, he noticed that cavalry twill and tweed sports jackets had gone down in the social scale whereas frayed jeans and dirty sweaters had gone up. Not an interesting and surely not an original observation. He suggested to William that this pub had become one to avoid.

'They all are. They're all full of people who've forgotten that we die.' He looked so gloomy as he said this that Edward laughed.

'Old age isn't so bad, if you consider the alternative.'

'Who said that?' asked William, interested.

'Maurice Chevalier.'

'How can these people die without looking silly?' William's eyeballs were moving slowly now, he was quietly drunk. 'They all spend too long choosing what to wear, what to drink, what to say – what kind of pub they want for Chrissake! Too much choice. We can't stand it. Suddenly they find it doesn't matter. None of it. What do they do? Who'd look most dignified dying? Charlie!'

'It might be hard to tell the difference.'

'So it should be. There used to be hardly any variation. What a relief! Wore the same kind of clothes all our lives, drank the same things in the same place. Never thought of changing. What's the point? So we spent our time among things calmly decaying, like ourselves. Most of our children died anyway. Now you can reach forty and get no nearer a real grief than the television news.'

'But that's better!'

'I'm not concerned with whether it's better or not! You've been too long away Edward, I shall have to take you in hand. I'm talking about what *is*. The embourgeoisification of all things!'

'A stage?' Edward raised his eyebrows to put the question in inverted commas.

'Quite,' said William obediently, turning away making a disappointed face. He would have liked to go on but he had gone on long enough. What he was saying was the commonplace of every social prophet from Cobbett to Karl Marx, but say it nowadays and the cry of reaction goes up. It stultified debate. Why shouldn't a man look coolly at the world and say what he sees! These changes, choices he'd been talking about *increased* the difficulties between men –

and yet they were mindlessly credited to be improvements! What's the use! Clearly he'd gone up a sidetrack that didn't interest Edward and anyway the women had arrived.

William watched them, surlily. They just stood, out of place, as were all the other women in the pub. Yet that was why the bloody place had been changed – to accommodate women! Women had still not learned how to behave if their arrival is not greeted by fuss, people getting up and so on. They didn't expect people to get up, not here anyway, but they didn't know what to do when nothing happened. And they never knew what they wanted to drink.

Edward played host, ordering drinks, grinning his wide social grin. William admired ease of manner and liked to watch it. He would like to have learned it but was usually too excited by something. He relaxed his defensive position at the bar and smiled towards them, noticing that Helen looked nondescript. She was wearing a mustard-coloured raincoat; a hand-me-down, William discovered later, from her mother. The lack of choosing, of insistence on choice, evidenced by her humbleness in wearing such a garment, would have pleased him if he had known; all he noticed was that it did nothing for her. Beryl, on the other hand, by a combination of beads, purple sweater with a collar almost up to her ears and a roughly napped navy-blue jacket, worn open, contrived to look both appropriate and chic. He was proud of her.

He left the three of them together, the evening must be rescued somehow. There was a man at the end of the bar whose wife had recently died. William liked him and knew, or thought he knew, what the man was feeling. He was standing quietly at the edge of an animated group, being taken out of himself by a group of talkative friends, and looking to William as though his self was being driven further and further into him, like a peg.

William touched him on the arm and he turned, half-away from the group. William, committed now, tried to gather himself, willing himself not to sway. He asked him how he was, how things were going, watching his diction. To his relief the man responded at once, talking of money, arrangements. But it was all right. He spoke as if his wife were still alive and they were going through this botheration together. Meanwhile his group of friends fell silent, eyeing William, who had a moment of panic. Though he was willing to carry his fellow-feeling through, go and visit this man, keep him company if that was what he wanted, he also wondered whether he was driving a wedge between him and his natural companions, who stood round, embarrassed as their friend mentioned the forbidden name. William had never pretended to himself that he understood the reactions of other men. Perhaps their evasions were necessary to them, and to give this newly bereaved man an opportunity to behave as he would have behaved himself was an imposition, would separate him from these people and so increase his isolation, not diminish it? From their silence this would seem to be so, yet the man himself had been turned into the interesting centre of the group, whereas before he had been silent at the edge of it. William wanted to teach them, but faltered. All his life he had refused the responsibilities of the teacher, mistrusted the possibility of one man consciously increasing the wisdom of another. It was this Edward had been talking about, he remembered, coming down the hill. It was true that in his books he left things open, undefined; he refused to insist, it was his nature. Suddenly, drunkenly, he felt the possibility of changing all that. He *would* teach them, insist, or try to. He would make up for his ridiculous failure of a conversation with Edward. He had energy to instil into these people.

The first thing was to change the pattern. For a wild moment he considered turning to the others and saying: 'What do *you* think of Doris's death?' but wisely rejected that idea. Then he saw the adjacent darts board was now not being used and suggested a game. His acquaintance accepted the idea and William turned to the others: 'Shall we make a foursome?' There was much discussion about partners, tossing of coins, ordering of drinks, and the game began; a natural transition made; William was triumphant. He smiled and chattered to the others, who answered briefly. Be damned to them.

His partner was his friend who turned out to be a practised player with an easy style, flicking the darts from his wrist and from just in front of his face, very relaxed. They won easily and it became an embarrassment, no other pair could knock them off the board and it was time

William went and joined his own group. He was pleased to see Beryl looking towards him, smiling, and more than pleased, delighted at the appropriateness, of Helen seated next to Charlie, turned squarely to him, whether talking or listening he could not be sure. Helen would see the point of Charlie and by God Charlie would see the point of Helen. He hoped Edward would not damp it for them. But Helen would not easily be damped.

At last it was over, William failed to get a final double and they were beaten. His friend put away his darts and pocketed them (if he had brought them he must have wanted to play so why had he not suggested that to his friends? William was always surprised at the tentative good manners of others). To his friends he said goodnight. There were protests, but he meant it, and anyway they were all involved and excited by the darts now. He gave the impression of a man who was returning to his new solitude because the time had come and he wanted to. 'I enjoyed that,' he said to William.

'So did I ... Keep going.'

'Oh, I dare say I shall. Thank you.' He looked at William, 'I'll drop by and see you one day on my way back from work. You still up at Berryman's?'

'Do it Tuesday. I'll be building a wall near the road.'

'I will if I can. I have some dahlia tubers. I could drop them in.'

The Indians of William's boyhood always brought gifts, put a formal distance between visitor and visited: excellent, sanitary idea. 'That would be marvellous,' said William, who preferred growing vegetables. In return he would ask him how to keep slugs off potatoes, this year when he had dug his up they were slimy, eaten hollow. If only he could remember this chap's name ...

Through the clouds of alcohol a spot of poison fell and spread as though his mind were blotting paper: what had he done, after all? Instigated a game of darts. You'd think he had saved the world! Yet the look of the man, and the promise of dahlia tubers, showed that he at least had recognized an attempt had been made. Because we bring so little is no reason for bringing nothing. The Indians knew that. He sat down, telling himself to be satisfied, and looked round the room. Beryl took his hand and gave it a squeeze.

'What *is* that chap's name?' he said.

'I don't know,' said Beryl. 'How's he taking it?'

'Not too badly. I'll ask Charlie.'

Charlie was sitting, upright as ever, with his eyes more bloodshot, staring unwaveringly at Helen.

'Charlie – what's the name of that chap who's just gone out?'

'Who?'

'Thick-set chap, short, curly hair.'

'Bill Hinds?'

Bill Hinds was tall and thin and bald and stood full in Charlie's line of vision.

'No. Grows dahlias. Lives in that cottage on the Weston crossroads.'

'Grows *dahlias* ...'

That was a dreadful piece of information to have given. Charlie would now go through the list of everyone local who grew dahlias, which was everyone. 'His wife was called Doris.'

'Ah. Doris Yardley.' Doris Yardley was the woman serving behind the bar, unmarried.

'No. You haven't quite got it Charlie. This Doris died.'

'Died?'

'Yes.'

'Ah.' He jerked his chin, pretending thought. Edward laughed. Charlie raised his head and looked at him politely.

'Never mind,' said William. 'It'll come to me.'

'Righto then,' said Charlie, and returned to his contemplation of Helen.

It was all very drab in this place, nothing much was happening. It was a relief to look at the colours of Beryl's clothes, but he noticed that underneath the slopped formica table she was clasping and unclasping her hands, rhythmically, though her face looked calm enough. Helen was flushed and amused by the attentions of Charlie and Edward was puffing his pipe, looking before him with lowered lids. There was a depressing amount still left in all their glasses.

Eventually, however, they were all outside, the women saying they were hungry and wanting to drive back, William and Edward agreeing to walk. It was cold and black and William craned his neck to receive as much of the cold as he could, it made a sensation of shapes on his patched cheeks, so that if he had drawn his face it would have appeared camouflaged, irregular blobs and squiggles of bracing cold among a kind of dullness. He raised his arms and waggled his fingers as they walked, as though trying to draw more of the air towards him.

'I don't know how you do it,' said Edward.

'Do what?'

'Exist on so little stimulation.'

William was experiencing, and had experienced, just about as much stimulation as he was capable of bearing, so he said nothing. Instead he began to run up the hill until he could go no further, and waited, panting, for Edward.

We don't really see anything, not properly, he thought, looking down at the road. It would probably be pretty overstimulating if we did. He continued this train of thought as he walked side by side with Edward up the last slope towards home. He had some difficulty keeping up, that run had been foolishness.

Then, as they rounded a corner, his heart nearly stopped, they were confronted by such a dreadful sight.

The crest of the hill was the flat horizon because the ground dropped away sharply on the other side. So as they climbed there appeared to climb out of the rim of hill in front of them a hedge, and in the middle of the hedge a gate, appearing bar by bar as they rose. And standing with its head over the gate, quite still, and looking at them, was an enormous monster.

A huge yellow head with bulging eyes and no body. William had a moment of terror, transported back to the beginnings when men never knew what dwarfing ghastliness they were going to meet round the next corner, the old dread that now only visits us in dreams. But even as he felt it he was realizing that what he was looking at, transformed by thin moonlight and the trick of its positioning on the horizon, body falling away, ears for some reason pressed back, was a horse. In fact not even a horse, a pony he knew well, its size exaggerated in proportion because it wasn't even looking over a gate but a small hurdle tied into the gap of the hedge.

How tremendous it had looked before he had known what it was! He had had to put it together piece by piece in his head – bulging eyes, hairy jaws, huge nostrils ... what *could* it be! Why, of course, it's Miss Hindley's pony Spring Corn! And as recognition came so did it shrink, so, as far as imagination and excitement were concerned, did it almost disappear. But that was just what he had been thinking, that we never really *saw* anything! Now, he couldn't see the pony, only a particular version of ponyness buried under his expectations of what ponyness is. Before, he had seen the thing itself, awful, inexplicable, an object of terror and worship. He had been in the position of the first man who saw the first horse. By God if we could see like that more often we wouldn't be bored!

The first horse! As they crossed the field to the cottage he kept turning back to look at the pony's head, still silhouetted against the sky above the hurdle, still catching a little moonlight, and he tried to bring back the terror of looking at it without understanding. He caught small echoes of it, but they grew less each time he looked.

Back at the house there was only one lamp still lit, in the kitchen. Beryl had gone to bed but Helen was waiting, yawning. Edward cut himself a slice of bread and a piece of cheese. 'I'll help you to get the generator working tomorrow,' he said, his mouth full.

William didn't feel hungry. 'You keep the lamp. I drank too much. Did you see that horse?'

'Yes.'

He waited, but Edward said no more. 'Good night.' He slowly climbed the familiar stairs, barely needing to feel his way, suddenly very tired.

Beryl made her small welcoming sound from beneath the bedclothes, between a purr and a grunt. William undressed quietly and climbed in beside her as carefully as he could.

He lay on his back and willed himself to dream; he wanted to get back to that horse country. Beryl touched his cheek with the tips of her fingers and then settled down to sleep again. He was grateful to her. 'Lord, Lord' he said to himself in the dark, out of gratefulness he wasn't sure for what precisely: for Beryl, for being alive, for the excitements he was feeling nowadays. 'Make me good' he said to himself in the dark, vaguely. Beryl felt close to him probably because he'd talked to that chap in the pub. And he did have something to offer. What he'd seen during his accident.

Maybe he'd died for a moment. Whatever it was he'd stood aside from himself and seen such good things. Calm and colour, that's what he'd felt, and seen. No judgement, no fret, only points of colour, and strands of it, in his own life and in other's lives, even people he did not know. These colours seemed to be moments of true response and the rest didn't matter, was colourless. And as though brooding over it all, like vast wings, was an enormous patience.

Certainly it made all the operations and so on easier to bear whilst they lasted. He still felt himself floating in those calm colours. He spoiled it all of course but his own backslidings never worried him. He was amazed at his own confidence in what he had seen, or dreamed. Sometimes he even approached it again, under an anaesthetic. By God he wasn't going to kick it out of himself because his mind told him to! Couldn't anyway. It was clamped inside him. An odd certainty beyond fret. Life, seen as a scene. Seen as serene.

Along the passage Edward was in bed beside the now sleeping Helen, thinking of William's books. There was always some holding back, he thought, reaching for a cigarette. Perhaps there had to be. Some of the later pieces were particularly quirky also, even curmudgeonly.

There was no ashtray by the bed so Edward half-opened a match-box and knocked the tip of his cigarette into it. He did not like smoking in bed; he would wake up in the morning with a taste in his mouth. He did not much like staying in this house. He got up, went to the window, and opened it slightly to let out the smoke. There was a thin rather tatty curtain attached directly to a wire like a spring and he pulled it back with difficulty. Across the field at the back the pony still stood at the gate, moving its head from side to side as though scratching its neck, but against nothing.

That had been an odd apparition earlier. He had felt William stiffen. Why had he said nothing? He turned away from the window impatiently and climbed back into bed. Why had *he* not said anything, but let the moment pass, waiting for William?

The truth was he did not share William's taste for mysteries, or his cosy capacity for love – if that was the word. Edward asked himself if he loved his own children.

After a moment's thought he decided that he did. But if they were killed in an air crash he would get over it. People did. Helen? He turned to look at her profile. Even in the dim light from the uncurtained window she was good to look at. Yes, he loved Helen. Of course. But he felt hopelessly unworthy. No, not unworthy, incompetent. Even the trustfulness of her just lying there sleeping irritated him. He felt that her whole weight was on him, he had to look after her and she was heavy and fragile. He felt he was a rather bendy tree into which a disproportionately large and beautiful bird had come to roost. No, he could not love her as she seemed to expect him to. He could not even, as a tree or as a man, support her.

Money, perhaps, would save them. If her aunt came across. Or her mother. He could hide behind the money; they would both enjoy it; and his own incapacities would not be so damned obvious. And yet the money would destroy him. He had not married Helen for that reason.

These were young man's thoughts and he grew impatient with them; he was no longer young. The trouble with him was boredom. God, that awful pub! He understood why William had drunk so much, forced those rather unwilling people into a game of darts. But he disliked the illusion, that William had seemed to be filled with when he came back to them, that he had made something happen. What? He'd merely used up some of his own energy. He should be more selfish and save his energy for his work.

That's all that mattered; preferably hard physical work so you fell into bed too exhausted to think. It would be all right once he got back to the farm. But the farm didn't pay and so was unreal, an opportunity, provided him by Helen, for tiring himself out.

Boredom. Nothing to do but wait for morning which would bring fresh energy and therefore a kind of hope. He looked at the confidently sleeping Helen and said 'Good night', stubbing out his cigarette with more violence than was necessary, half-hoping she would wake. But she did not, thereby saving him from hinting that he needed comfort, therefore from receiving it, and as a result feeling even more irritated with himself.

5

In the months that followed it slowly dawned on William that what Edward had meant, what held him back, was embarrassment. This surprised him; it was indeed an English disease. And anyway his work had always been so unfashionable, so determinedly out of what reviewers regarded as the main stream that he had always regarded himself as more defiant than shy.

Nowadays his reputation seemed to have taken a turn upwards again. He was visited occasionally by young people. He noticed that as opinions of his importance rose, so did his financial resources dwindle. Books were written about his books but this had no effect on his sales and it was ages since he had written anything new.

He enjoyed the visits of admirers on the whole. If they were young they gave the impression that they found the way he lived less mysterious than his coevals did, but he was aware of disappointing them. They seemed to expect some rule of life from him, like a code of hygiene. He refused to give it to them, of course, but even so their departure, slightly puzzled, left him with a distinct sense of phoniness, of having said too much.

Was he embarrassed? Was he giving them short measure? Did his belief that certain things were not talked about, because of the risk of talking nonsense, do a disservice to those things? Far from being protected by that delicate silence, did their importance, unasserted, unargued, shrink to vanishing point?

God was a word, a concept that had always particularly embarrassed William in public. He believed in Him, always had, and never once in his writings had he said so.

There were many reasons for the omission – a dislike of boring people prominent among them. What the kids wanted from him was some kind of explicit statement *with reasons*. How awful! He couldn't possibly give them that because he was unsure what they were, could not think of them as *reasons* anyway. Nevertheless he did believe in Him, capital letter and all, and believed that He looked down on him, William, and on everybody else, with love and understanding and even, on occasion, and in answer to prayer, gave help.

He could not say that. Why not, if it was what he believed?

Because he was frightened of sounding an even sillier old fool than he doubtless was. It was late in the day to come to that conclusion. Surely, to think otherwise was an invitation to go even further in the direction of yesterday morning.

He thought about the previous morning and tried to remember more of that brief exchange with Edward six months before. It must have been precisely this holding-back that Edward had sensed, and it was this new position, a desire to speak out without shame, that he had been trying to describe. What a lot of time we waste before we know that we really mean what we say. It had needed the shock that morning to bring him to his senses.

Reading the paper after breakfast he had come across a review of a collection of his old pieces. It had taken him by surprise because he had forgotten they were being reissued, but the real shock-value lay not so much in what the reviewer had said about his work but in the surrounding article where his own little notice lay buried.

It was, surprisingly, an article religious, specifically Christian, in tone, and he had been reading it with complacent approval. The reviewer had even quoted a woman who particularly interested William, Simone Weil – 'the world is God's language to us' – and William, in mid-nod of agreement, and in the midst of contentedly thinking this defined precisely his own attitude to the world which he had spent his life expressing in his work, came upon his own name, with the jump of excitement the sight of his own name in print still gave him, only to discover that this reviewer, regretfully, lumped him on the other side! Among those who did not think thus, to whom the material world was all!

William had been stunned. Not hurt, not indignant, appalled. The worst was that this reviewer, whom he knew slightly, had been responsible as an editor for printing some of these pieces in the first place. William had always therefore regarded him as a man who understood them. He had clearly not understood them at all. Who in the world, in that case, did?

William wrote to him at once; a friendly letter to relieve his own feelings, pointing out his bewilderment. It had not been a successful letter. There was only one passage in which William felt he was getting near to the point. He had quoted someone – was it Henry James? – "Don't *tell* me, *show* me." 'But what,' he had gone on, 'when I try to *show*, if I seem to *tell* nothing?'

To be so old, so practised, and so incompetent!

It was now early Spring. In the months that had passed since Edward and Helen's visit nothing much had happened, to outward seeming, except Beryl's trouble. In fact it had been a time of turmoil and great excitement. Feeling, not always very specific feeling, built up pressure inside him as though he was a boiler. If he had any sense he would fear for his own reason – the Irishness of the idea pleased him – never mind Beryl's.

Yesterday morning he had walked where he was walking now, along the side of a high field bordered by a tangled wood that fell away sharply down a steep bank. It had been a grey, windy day but the wood sheltered him. He knew the force of the wind because of the great noise it made in the tops of the trees, they swished and swayed and creaked. He had sat at the top of the bank looking down into the dark wood; the sky above it was dark and the trunks of the beech trees were silver against it, weaving in the wind, their top branches crackling against each other. It was all a series of greys which became more and more brilliantly contrasted as he watched. Then he lowered his eyes and they fell on the first undergrowth of the year, fresh green, a humble plant he knew to be called dog's mercury, but so highly coloured against the tones of the greys, so unmoving below the waving and scratching of the upper branches, such tender green stillness under the rushing and tearing of the wind, that he fell into a kind of trance. And, half in that trance and half out of it, he found himself reciting, very slowly, which is a trick he had learned from Simone Weil, the words of the Lord's Prayer. Then he had slept for a moment and that was how he had spent the first part of his morning.

He would never write about that because it was insufficiently interesting. But nothing was of greater importance to him. Therefore his writing had ceased to interest him.

He sat again in the same place. He had said the Lord's Prayer, that satisfactory collection of words, because he was undergoing an experience far removed from his own concerns, one which included, and transcended even, the world's pain. It was a wholly serious moment. And he was grateful for it. Yes, there was no getting round it, he had said the prayer out of gratefulness, for grey trees and green undergrowth. Self, *feeling* ... No. There was as little self as was possible to him in his feeling. And the prayer is all 'us' and 'we', no 'I', no wanting in it, except for a clearer feeling.

He considered Huxley's absurd idea that a response to a beneficent nature was a Western European illusion not shared by those who lived in 'real' nature, where snakes bit and tigers ravened. He had lived in such places and knew Huxley to be wrong. Men everywhere raised their eyes to the stars to as much purpose, at least, as Huxley's Shelleyized Englishmen, parading in tweeds to admire the sunset.

Was he then to feel ashamed in public (he had no private shame) of universal sensations because they were experienced at the edge of a harmless wood in the Midlands? Could he not write about it? Did he have to explain that although he had recited the Lord's Prayer he was neither Catholic nor Protestant nor for that matter Muslim or Buddhist or anything else, but he simply believed in God (and, astonishing fact, impenetrable to analysis now, believed as it happened in Christ because his mother had taught him to, and among much he had been taught that he had thrown away he retained that because it had always fitted his experience like a key, opening more and more doors further and further into mysteries until his head swam – but Christ himself had said he was the Way, not the destination); was he to go into all that?

To hell with England! He'd write one more book, putting it all down, it would doubtless be bad, and then he would shut up. After that he would go wherever he was pushed. He hoped they would push him somewhere, that he would not merely be forgotten, stepped over. That would be hard on Beryl because he would need money. Beryl might have to be looked after ...

He lay back on the bank as he had done the previous morning, using his cap as a pillow, closed his eyes and tried to stand outside Beryl, so that he could encompass her trouble separately from himself, so that he could help her. He had a sense of his arms stretching, of standing in their sitting room, each of his arms outstretched and still growing, ten feet long, as he strove to include her fish-like dartings to the rim of her bowl, which was his arms. He could stretch no further, she escaped, her eyes furtive, her hair ugly, to sink in a corner, huddled against a wall, filled with a dry sobbing, terrified of him and of everything. This had happened twice now, since the night of the wind. What he must guard against – if only he could get outside her and see her as suffering, afflicted, not merely as rejecting him – was the temptation he had had when she had done this to sink in an opposite corner, also huddled, as mad and as angry as she.

Because she filled him with terror too. He could accept and even enjoy the indifference of the non-human world. But malevolence, which did not exist in nature, was another matter. If a loved person was involuntarily filled with it, for chemical reasons or whatever, it cut at the root of everything. It implied that he had only been able to avoid being overwhelmed by an awareness of the torture-chambers of the world because he was lucky, and perhaps because he had chosen to live in complacent ignorance outside the prison gates. It made his whole life a nonsense.

Lying back with his eyes closed he heard the crunch of more than one pair of feet on the dry twigs at the side of the wood, and voices which stopped, because whoever it was had seen him. He turned his head on the bank and opened his eyes. It was his landowner the Admiral, and his bailiff, walking along the field edge towards him.

He decided not to jump to his feet, it would look too shifty. Nor could he lie there. He sat up and turned in their direction, smiling. 'Good morning,' he said, first.

They did not reply. William decided not to speak again until they did.

They approached and looked down. 'Nice mornin',' said the Admiral.

William agreed, climbing to his feet. The three of them stood in silence, smiling. He was struck once again by the handsomeness of his landlord, small, compact, very confident. His bailiff, whom William suspected would have cut anyone's throat for tuppence, had a neck much wider at the back than at the front.

'Doin' a spot of composin'?'

'That sort of thing.'

'Good spot for it.'

'Yes.'

Relations between them had long dried up. When William had first rented the cottage he had conscientiously tried to fill his landlord with some of his own protectiveness towards trees. 'Absolutely lovely,' said the Admiral, sharing with William the view of a particularly fine beech-hanger for which William had fears. Within a week it was clear-felled, replaced by neat rows of christmas trees. 'Like the new plantation?' the Admiral had said, grinning.

Now that small hard man girded himself again for conversation, 'Wife all right?'

'Fine thank you. Yours?'

The Admiral seemed startled at the question. There was a slight pause. 'Cracking form,' he said, eventually.

'Splendid!' said William, regretting how instantly infectious the lingo was. He was of no account in his landlord's eyes and never would be. The Admiral owned everything in sight.

'How are the crops doing?' said William, forced into speech by another of their long silences.

'Very well. Very well. Eh John?'

'Very well.'

'Good.' William tried to stifle in himself a certainty that the bailiff was gloating at him from behind his employer's shoulder. He almost certainly was gloating but William suspected himself of social paranoia.

'Need any repairs done to the cottage?' said the Admiral, putting on a concerned expression.

'No, thank you.' William's one request for repairs, justified by his lease, had been received with such unspoken amusement, and had taken so long in the outcome, that William had done them himself. He had resolved not to put himself in that position again.

The Admiral seemed genuinely astonished at this lack of petitioning by a tenant and fastened his pale blue eyes on

William in a nonplussed, unseeing fashion.

'You haven't a dog with you, have you?'

'No.'

'We've some pheasants in these woods. Don't want them disturbed.'

'I haven't a dog.'

'Well then ...'

'Well.'

They broke it up, relieved, and William continued on his way, which he chose to be the opposite of theirs, although it took him in a direction he had not intended. He felt disturbed and scruffy.

He would not tell Beryl of the conversation. Early in their marriage he had enjoyed reciting his failures to her because he found them, in the main, amusing. But they made her impatient. She was always full of what he should have said, clearly misunderstood his pleasure in all inadequacies, his own as well as other's, and in the end he had seen that she was right. One either had something positive to report or one remained silent. He regretted this; he would have enjoyed making a saga out of this encounter, imitating the Admiral, exaggerating his own hangdog appearance, bits of twig sticking to the back of his hair, caught kipping at the edge of the wood. Beryl preferred her mind's eye to be filled with a more glamorous image of himself, which proved, he supposed, that her normal picture of him was not all that attractive or secure. If he had been praying, for instance (not that he would ever have told her that, she would have laughed, a reaction of hers he also approved of, but there were occasions when he chose to avoid it), she would have had him kneeling like a St Jerome, an unambiguous figure behaving unambiguously, even to the boiled blue eye of the Admiral. At least, then, she seemed strongly to feel, each would know where the other stood – or knelt.

Quite right. She really was much more masculine than he was.

The trouble is that Beryl, and others as forthright, would never find herself praying at the edge of a wood and therefore would never be so found. This made all her pronouncements about correct behaviour on such occasions invalid. Whereas those who are given to such self-forgetful extravagances learn early all sorts of evasions and concealments, otherwise they might have found themselves driven out of the herd altogether.

She always wanted him to expostulate with the Admiral about his felling policy. But you cannot talk to such men. They inhabit different planets. To make a row of staring stumps, thick as a gamekeeper's arm, out of hawthorns, hazels, wild plum, in order to save a quarter of an acre in a mile, was the action of a man to whom there is no appeal. Anyway, he didn't even increase the size of the field. The margin beneath the amputated stumps was as nettly as ever and sprouting thickly with the frustrated suckers of these mutilations.

Nor was this the end. On the night of the wind the magnificent trees below them had all gone over. Long ago the hedge had been exactly set, to protect them. Unshielded they had been torn out of the ground, their root systems still intact, a huge circle of neat turf around their roots standing up vertical like an opened lid ...

In fact he quite liked the Admiral. He was a piece of nature himself, like a hawk, or a stoat, his vision as narrow as his appetite.

William walked with his head bent, glaring down at his boots. You can't just croon over a scene like a picture on a calendar! Beryl was puzzled by his attitude; she thought he cared and then, at some outrage, she seemed to find he didn't. But there's no lament in nature. It either fights back, or goes round, emerging again in another form, or it dies. On it goes, never back. He would do the same. If other men wanted to destroy all that was non-man they would. Belly-aching was ridiculous. William assured himself there was no point in being in a temper with the world.

A tractor was dragging a bright red sprayer over the green shoots of the corn. A pair of lapwings who had fancied it safe to nest at such a season, as it would have been a year or two before, were protesting. One of them kept flopping in front of the tractor, feigning a broken wing.

William doubted whether the tractor driver could hear their cries, or even see them. After hours in the cab, drivers had a shocked, deadened look. So he would not even know he was driving them away. If they had laid already the tractor was probably going over their eggs. It would certainly be easy to become depressed.

He opened the door of the cottage quietly because he did not want to meet Beryl just then. When he had left the house earlier they had not been in sympathy.

She limped slowly from the sitting room to the kitchen as he was hanging his things up in the cubby-hole by the door. She passed quite close to him but she did not look at him, nor did she speak. She was capable of that sort of non-encounter, meaning no punishment by it, but William was not, he was always horrified.

Beryl hoped he would not follow her into the kitchen. Her back towards the door, her eyes shut, she willed him not to. But behind her came the flap-flap of heavily booted feet. She had been half-reading, re-reading mindlessly, an old magazine, and had pushed it away guiltily when she heard him come in, furious at herself for behaving like that, with him for making her. She had long periods when her mind idled, a sort of non-life, very comfortable, and she enjoyed it. She had always been like this. There were parts of her girlhood, looking back, that seemed to have passed almost wholly in a non-receptive trance, and she was not ashamed of it. When she did respond, she did so fully and she needed these interludes, it seemed to her. Anyway, that's the way she was, so why should William make her feel guilty about it? Why could he not just leave her alone?

He had four ways of reacting when he caught her out in this way – why could he not simply take no notice, just *go away* – he was either reproachful, or puzzled, or impatient, or compensatingly over-brisk – 'What's to be done? Ah, the housework. You sit down, I'll do it' – that sort of thing.

She busied herself with some washing-up, making too much clatter, feeling him behind her back. She guessed it was the puzzled approach today. She turned round with what she intended as a cheerful smile on her face.

'Had a nice walk?'

Her expression froze William to the spot, it was a frightful grimace.

'Yes thank you.' He fiddled sightlessly with some letters on the dresser. They had arrived with the newspaper before he left the house. He had no wish to open them. He tried a chuckle: 'You make me sound like an old gent who takes a morning constitutional!'

She resisted the temptation to say: Aren't you? Don't you? Only when unendurably pressed did Beryl say anything wounding. She respected William's relentless self-communings, after all he had his life to live. Her only beef was, as she put it to herself, turned back to the sink, that he expected her to live his life as well, rebuking her by implication for stuffing indoors, imploring her by hints to look out of the window, or to go out and peer into the bottom of a ditch and there find a cure for all her 'troubles'. That cured William's troubles and good luck to him but she knew that she either responded to her surroundings intensely, so intensely that William, in his steady way, was sometimes dismayed, or she didn't respond at all. Indeed, to look in a ditch or wherever it was William wanted her to look, and see nothing of interest left her worse off than before, more self-enclosed – if that is what she was.

'Penguin's are doing the most obscure works nowadays in their Classics series.' William had picked up a paperback from the untidy dresser.

'Oh no.'

'Yes, people I've never heard of.'

'I can't say they've ever done anyone I've never heard of.'

William's desire was to rush off to W.H. Smith's and bring back a pile she couldn't possibly have known about. Instead he stood there, checked, and Beryl suddenly felt extremely tired. 'I think I'll go and lie down.'

'Yes, do.' To take as much rest as Beryl did was not far off being dead.

'Are you going to work this morning?'

'Of course.' If work meant paper covered, ideas satisfactorily expressed, he glumly doubted it.

'There's a bit of cheese in the larder for your lunch I think.'

'Fine.'

He looked forlorn. 'Dear William,' she said. 'You want all your stories to have happy endings, don't you.'

'I suppose I do,' he said woodenly, not understanding. He would certainly have liked her to sound more confident that there was indeed some cheese for his lunch. Anyway, it was Beryl who disliked hearing tales of failure. But he suspected she meant something more than that, something about them.

'It's not like that, not really,' she went on, at the door. 'There are dull patches. People are – different,' she ended lamely, not quite understanding what she was trying to say, or how to express to him that his sense of their daily life together had become over-simple.

'You make me sound rather hearty,' he said.

'You are a bit. Never mind.'

'Never mind! Hearty!'

'I didn't mean that. I mean it doesn't matter.'

'Oh.' William decided to leave it there, not wanting an argument or to hear his character analysed. 'Did you see that review of my book in yesterday's paper?' he said, astonished at himself.

'What book?'

'The reprint they're doing. D'you remember? I told you.'

'Oh. Yes. No.'

'Would you like to?'

'Yes.'

'It's nothing much.' He handed the paper which he had detected underneath the empty fruit bowl. At least it was empty of fruit but contained knitting, some worrying-looking bits of a dismantled electric light plug and a leaking tube of glue.

She too was surprised at him being so doggy, passing her his little bones received from the outside world. Did he still expect her admiration? In which case in spite of the mess she seemed to be in she was the stronger. For she did not expect his admiration, not at all. There was nothing in her to admire and if there were it would be worthless if she became aware of it. Surely William must accept himself by now? But he had not even been able to accept Peter growing up ...

She took the paper and went upstairs, leaving William himself to wonder why he had given her such a flavourless morsel. It seemed as though he had been forced to give her something that proved his existence outside this kitchen, perhaps a little superior to the constitutional-taking fuddy-duddy she seemed to think him. But the piece in the paper suggested that he was precisely that!

He bleakly regarded the half-finished pile of washing up. Beryl had simply abandoned it in mid-task because she felt like a rest. There was something grand about that. Beryl had always had style.

He rolled up his sleeves and began to finish it. The good thing about Beryl was that you always knew where you were with her. Probably not where you would like to be but there was no pretending. You need never be in doubt as to what she was thinking – except all the time ..., he suddenly said to himself, pausing with a dish under the hot tap, held at the edge so he would not scald his fingers. No, what was good about her was, he clarified to himself, holding another plate in the same way – there seemed to be about three days' washing-up here, surely they hadn't used all these dishes! – she never did anything she didn't want to. Very restful. She either did something, or she didn't. In this case, he sighed at the sink, she didn't. She wouldn't be grateful to him for finishing the washing-up, or resentful if he didn't finish it. She would simply take it for granted that he had done what he wanted to, as she had done.

He remembered the reason for the washing-up. His literary agent and his wife had come over for supper last night, staying at some grander house nearby. They were nice enough people. He liked old Billy, though his unqualified admiration for William, or at least his pretence of it, which he appeared to regard as part of his professional duty, was a bit exhausting. His wife Gillian was pleasant too, intelligent, sat in a long Victorian dress very upright, with a little lace collar round her long neck, smiling all evening. William remembered nothing of the occasion except a nearly overwhelming desire to leave the room in order to cut his toenails.

Why shouldn't he do the washing-up! And, while he was about it, why should he expect the provision of a bit of cheese? He went to the larder to check on the cheese, leaving the hot tap running, and there was some, he had to admit that, though it consisted of a cheerless amount of rind. Really, why couldn't Beryl ...! He stopped himself and went back to the sink, stopping also a foolish determination to do the shopping, thereby ensuring the household a decent supply of decent cheese. Last time, in a huff, he had done that, he had been so surprised by the sudden rise in the price of everything that he had resolved to live on bread and water rather than be caught in the 'inflationary spiral'. But caught he was, The Admiral would be sure to raise the rent of this slum when their lease came to an end. Maybe the reprint of his book would sell. Which reminded him of the dismal little notice he had passed on to Beryl.

It looked like a dreary afternoon ahead, Beryl asleep upstairs, he in his study glooming over that false start of a poem. He noticed the plates he had put on the rack were dirty underneath where they had been stacked, he would have to do them again. No, he wouldn't go upstairs and visit her in bed; she had not seemed in that mood at all and he didn't fancy being snubbed at the moment. This holding under the tap business didn't seem to be working, there was too much washing-up to do and the hot water was running tepid. He found an apron over the back of a chair and tied it on, filled a plastic basin, added washing-up liquid, and began again at the beginning. He saw the floor of the kitchen was none too clean either, where he had splashed it and trodden in mud from his shoes. He would do that too. He began to enjoy himself, polishing the plates carefully. After all, Beryl did this everyday and he wandered around thinking she was idle. He must help out more often. Better than work. First he'd have a bite to eat. He went to the larder and got out the cheese, looking around for some bread. There was none. Really, Beryl ... He contented himself with a rather soft biscuit, planning his assault on the floor.

Upstairs Beryl lay on their high bed. The newspaper was on the dresser, forgotten; she had not brought up her glasses anyway. Colourless light came through the small window which was shut to reduce the noise of the enormous tractors that thundered in all the fields around their house. She wanted to crawl to the bottom of the bed under the bedclothes, their relentless banging and roaring, so patient, so unstoppable, bore her down. The energy of it! The prevision! Now is the time for sowing, rolling, spraying, so that we may have crops in four months' time. In the early morning farm machinery was made ready, there was clanking of attachments, bruised fingers, shouting of orders, and then for the rest of the day, and innumerable days following, men sat in their high machines, muffs on their ears, crisscrossing the high empty fields in an envelope of din.

It appalled her. The hope of it, the patience of it. But now for a moment she was out of all that, or was trying to be; was just a woman, a body, a long picture show of previous versions of herself. She dreamed, waking, about her past, savouring it without regret, letting her mind go where it wanted to and making no judgement: out of the judging world of men who made of themselves previsioning machines, clearing the dust of the past, making dispositions for the future. That was inadequate, suffocatingly superficial. She pottered around inside herself instead because only there, somewhere, was food; and all her thoughts were enclosed inside that noise.

It had been the noise of the wind that had broken her, weeks ago, for the first time, though she had sensed the breakdown, just as she had sensed the approach of the wind. It was the noise of the wind and the meaningless, mindless movement of it. All day it had blown, making the cottage creak and doors rattle; at first twigs had been hurled off branches but by the afternoon it had been the branches themselves that sailed gracefully across the fields; a lean-to shed by the barn along the road had collapsed with a slow, tearing crash and pieces of black corrugated iron had floated on the wind, horizontal, stalling, balancing on the sheer force of it. At first she had thought they were rags of black plastic as she watched, fearful, from inside the house, then she saw that supported on the air like wings was hard jagged iron. It was unendurable.

It was unendurable but she endured it. A wind scouring the surface of the world like a great sea, taking everything with it, making her press her hands against the wall to steady herself, clutch at the floor with her toes in terror. But then at night, William sleeping, it had really come. She listened to the terrible roaring above the roof, hearing tiles torn off, the chimney pot topple and bounce down the roof smashing on the concrete outside. It was horrible, but still it grew, as though enraged, until it became more than a wind, it became a noise heard in a fever, a delirium of noise, a squadron of gigantic aeroplanes aimed directly at the house, there came a particular moment when they were sure to hit, two monstrous squadrons must have met and formed a wedge driving straight into her head. There was no escape, it was aimed straight at her, not a gusting roar

People and Weather

but a growing, deep-throated baying, irresistible, implacable, final. She fled.

She ran out of the house with the terrible noise in the dark above her, around her, tearing at her. The cold of it was like teeth, it blew her down, she scrambled up, her feet gashed by stones, she fled across the field, threw herself at a hedge hardly feeling the pain of the thorns, felt the force of her screaming in her body but in the noise of the wind only heard a feeble useless noise coming out of her. She was mad.

It was quite something to think she had been mad. She lay and remembered that night and knew if it happened again she would go mad again because it was maddening. For her it had been the only response possible. She had known the wind and what it meant. To have endured it would have been to pretend it was something less than it was, which was utterly, indifferently hostile.

Control was valueless in the face of something so enormous and she had relished her loss of holding-together, the relinquishment of pretence; she was a hopelessly vulnerable rag of screaming flesh stretched across thorns and there had been luxury in the release of it, the appropriateness.

She heard William moving about downstairs. She heard the clank of a bucket, the squeezing of a mop into a pail. He was clearing up.

She thought of her mother who, it was more than possible, had in the closing years of her life thought of nothing whatsoever but her house. Did she now, as her mother would have said, 'have too much time to *think*?' What a contemptible attitude to life! However true, however prudent, she would have none of it. What sort of a notion was it, that we lived best at a remove from our true selves! It was true that when we delved deep there were danger-signals set off in the head. So be it.

But on one thought her mind jagged, as though on a spike.

Once having surrendered control, as on the night of the wind, it had become easier, a positive temptation, to do so again. It had contained a deliciousness. It had been *right* ...

William's frightened face bending over hers: 'It's all right,' he kept saying, 'It's all right,' putting his face close as though smelling her, so that she could hear what he said without his having to shout the consolation like a madman, against the noise of the wind.

'Then take away the wind,' she had said, quite calm now, watching him from a distance, inside herself, as though cast up drowned on a shore and William a swimmer still, deluded that he could yet save himself. She watched him look about for something to wrap round her head to cut out the wind noise, watched him hesitate for a second before he took off his dressing-gown to bury her head in it, keeping her mouth free, and her eyes. She wanted to see, she did not want to close her eyes. She was Ariel watching Ferdinand and Miranda, Stephano and Trinculo, even Prospero, with the same unfeeling incomprehension. What she no longer had was fellow-feeling. She noted his nightshirt straining like a flag on the pole of his body, she noted he must be cold. He knelt to try and lift her from the lee of the hedge where she had fallen and she did not help, lay, like an awkward sack. She giggled as she remembered this. How awful she had been! William, kneeling again, gathering her up, losing her, gathering up parts of her again, straining to rise, had fallen on top of her in the mud. They had both lain there a moment and then he had tried again to lift her, dragging her ankles on the ground, grazing them, digging his fingers and chin painfully into her, struggling to gain a grip. She had made no effort to adjust herself, to help him and to save herself pain. It had not seemed worth it. She was beyond pain. She knew, at the same time, that William was doing what he had to do and that what he did was irrelevant. She would have been content to continue to lie where she was. They got back somehow. William, gasping, dropped her heavily into a chair and then collapsed himself, his forehead on the arm of it.

'The wind hates us,' she said.

She listened to William panting and then he said with difficulty, his forehead still on the arm of the chair 'The wind neither hates us nor loves us. It is indifferent.'

'That's it! The whole world is indifferent' – and here you began to cry, Beryl said to herself, and that was false. False! Behaving as an hysterical woman might behave when you were still a drowned body on the shore, quite dead, watching William chafe your feet, cover your scratches with

Vaseline, making little clicking noises with his tongue at their apparent painfulness of which you felt nothing except a quite pleasant burning, watching his hands shake.

'You love the wind,' you said and William had replied, looking up, 'It's you I love, not the wind,' and you pretended to be pleased, whereas although you understood the words they meant nothing to you, and you despised William for the ease with which he said them and his apparent confidence in their importance. How cunning you were, pretending like that, watching yourself on the shore, cold and perfect as a pebble, and William foolishly still in the water! He had gone on then, said we must expect no help from the world, only men could help each other which is why men *must* help each other and why we, Beryl and William, must help each other. It was all meaningless to Beryl, and absurd; as she lay on her shore she saw something far beyond human clinging-together, beyond love, beyond death even. She had glimpsed a supreme, indifferent coldness, which was supremely inviting.

Then William said something that caught her attention. First she said 'But you love the world. You're always watching it and writing about it. How can you love it if it doesn't love you?'

He had looked at her, as though he had been cleaned, almost flayed by the wind, and by exhaustion, the bones of his face very clear and his voice unusually certain.

'I love it *because* it doesn't love me. It is more interesting than I am.'

Just for a moment, staring at him, she understood what he meant.

The understanding vanished, or lost its edge almost at once, but she remembered how impressed by William she had suddenly been. As though this cold pocket of death she lived inside, looking out with confidence not only because no worse could befall her but because nothing could reach her at all, was, she suddenly saw, something William already *contained*, unsuppressed, lived and bumbled around, even drew nourishment from. Whereas she was trapped inside. For the first time since the wind had driven her from the house she sensed the possibility of recovery; not just a settling into a routine the object of which was to stop her thinking, but some sort of genuine recovery in which the sense of desolation was not denied but admitted, and used; a starting-point; not, as she had imagined, a personal discovery of the hollowness of all things but a knowledge of our misery which, because it was real, contained the possibility of real laughter.

She remembered all this, smiling, lying on her bed. She remembered how tired she had suddenly felt and how long she had slept.

She had been tired ever since. There was a chance she was using her 'condition' to punish William. Her frequent irritations with him did not always derive from it; on the contrary, they were more often perfectly ordinary pieces of bad temper which she tried to dignify by connecting them with what was, she supposed, her 'clinical' depression.

The machines had stopped. She became aware of the lull – it must be their tea-break – and climbed off the bed to look out. She stood at the window her elbows on the sill, her chin cupped in her hands, her bottom stuck out into the room; a young girl's position. It was an ordinary lightless April day. William had stopped clanking about downstairs. In a moment she would go down to make them both some tea. Why not? The cloud cover was level and intact, not dark and threatening rain, just steadily exclusive of varieties of light. Nevertheless, on the dull hedge that lined the road at the back she could make out the beginnings of a green blush; a particularly handsome sycamore was turning yellow and pink, and in the field to the right, she could just see by craning, the new green wheat was showing well. A hawk with still wings like little curved swords flashed across her eyeline. The English Spring went on as usual, unlit, cold, difficult to notice unless you went about peering like William which was a bit self-conscious. Just then the clouds parted, not very dramatically but at least there was an edge to one bank of the sky and a hole through which was visible not blue exactly but a slightly more colourful grey. Immediately the sycamore looked more yellow and more pink, the hedge had a more decided powdering of green and all the shapes, both in the ground, the swell and fall of it, and in the growing things, became clear in outline, unique in personality. It was a pleasing picture and Beryl felt a touch of pleasure. She went to the mirror, pulled up the cane-seated chair and began to brush her hair.

William's hair was standing on end, his hands still soft and tingling, smelling scented from the washing-up liquid. He was gazing down in irritation at the morsels of his poem, for the hundredth time asking himself what was missing in it.

The noise of the machines had made him restless, and now the sound of Beryl moving about upstairs made him fear that his time for uninterrupted work was coming to an end and, yet again, nothing done. The absurd thing was that he was attempting to describe something that happened last spring and in the process of doing so was locked away from the observation of this one. All writing had that absurdity at its heart: you have to remove yourself from experience, sometimes even deny yourself new material, in order to write at all.

He enjoyed the bustle of the machines. It annoyed him to have to block it out. This was the most interesting time of the year to be outside.

Rubbing his eyes hard, revolving his fists in either socket, he began again: last year about this time, he read, looking at his notes, he had stood 'in the hollow centre of a bush – a series of bushes, a thicket – on a cold northern slope. Nothing was out yet, nothing stirring' ... and he had seen colours.

Pale grey grass, uneaten by the sheep the year before because of the bramble thorns. And at the low heart of the bush was an extraordinary green on the stems so that if you narrowed your eyes there seemed a steady, emerald-coloured smoke around its centre. This was green lichen covering the damp low-down stems of the bush and it steadily changed its tone as the bush rose until it ceased, imperceptibly, and had become a faint purple, the stems' true colour, as the bush spread and sprayed, covering its green smoke-heart in a smoky purple hood. There were still leaves on the bramble, a leathery dead green, mottled, rimmed with blotches like old blood. Old nests spilt green moss and auburn feathers. Then he saw movement: a rabbit with myxomatosis, blind, its head puffed and suppurating, lurching, half-falling, sensing his presence and seeking the shelter of the bush it could not see.

It lurched against some yellow rocks.
Too horrible for buzzard or fox.

And the blood around its eyes was like the blood-stains on the brambles, they toned together. The sky was cold blue. There was a sudden great noise and four jet planes, painted red, tightly wing-tip to wing-tip, swept along the valley and rose, turning on their sides, then on their backs, flying upside down, the bubbles of their cockpit hoods glinting. They were so confident! He thought of the young men inside them, as young as Peter, possibly with small moustaches. How confident they seemed above the burning bush whose colours they would never know – somehow their redness proved they would never have time to watch that slow unfolding – above the terrible rabbit and himself, nestling in the forgotten fur of the world!

The airmen were his representatives. He profited from their mastery. The rabbit was his responsibility also, poisoned so that it should not eat the crops. There was blood around its eyes, as there seemed to be blood on the bramble leaves.

But it was not a horror scene. It was incomprehensible however, he could not bring it all together. What he felt, what entered him, and what existed outside himself independent of his feelings, was the patience of the bush, its colours slowly burning along the fuses of its stems, disappearing upwards into the sky, a devoted homage to the light. A ladder, that rose upwards beyond the sky, connecting earth with heaven, reaching patiently beyond him, beyond the rabbit, up past the confident young men in their bright noisy machines. The bush might be grubbed out tomorrow. It was only tolerated in this unconsidered spot because nothing else would usefully grow. But it existed, now, with warm colour, colossal, contained force and – patience. There was an angel in the burning bush and it spoke to him, of patience. He could not carry the angel away, it lived in the bush and he was cold and had to leave but he left afflicted; not with the indifference of the world to himself, but because it was charged with colour and homage and indifferent to his praise, that's all. Returning home he tried to express this, and failed.

A year later he was still trying. Better give up. He was wasting his time.

He sighed; he would like to live like the bush, gratefully receiving colour, sending it back. Beryl was making tea in the kitchen. He'd go and join her.

He stood up and leaning on his fingers, looked down at the pieces of paper on the table. Perhaps he should leave out the rabbit. It tended to dominate. No, it was a part of the picture. The aeroplanes too. They had frightened sleepy pigeons out of trees, they'd fallen like plump stones, only remembering to use their wings when they were clear of the bare ash branches.

He remembered those ashes no longer existed. They had been blown down in the wind. One had fallen right across that bush, flattening it.

Much had happened because of that wind.

He remembered the quick cold of the water through his night shirt as he knelt to lift her. That night he had felt an infantile tenderness towards them both. In that dreadful noise and extreme cold, extreme at least to him in thin flannel, wet-kneed, in the dark, he had a strong sense of huddlement, of just the two of them against the world, Babes in the Wood, the weight of their years together on each of them, like a coat – or, better, like a skin. It seemed to him immeasurably valuable, their one true possession; he had seldom felt so married. It was pleasurably infantile because of the warmth and exclusiveness and, yes, the security. Security, out in that black roaring field with Beryl clearly, at least temporarily, out of her mind.

He looked at her now, over his mug of tea. She was better, or she seemed to be. There would be recurrences, of course. There had been already; fits of silent weeping; that terrible slow slide down the wall till she huddled by the skirting.

She had really frightened him in the field. It was the quality of the look she had given him when, bent over her in the dark he could see her eyes, as though she saw him clearly without any tie of affection or familiarity, even of human sympathy. Even hatred, fear, is some form of connection. To look at another person de-personalized is no look at all, therefore she did not see him, not truly. But that she was capable of such a looking ...

Sitting at the table in the small, not very light kitchen, with its window that gave onto the bank, he felt again her small body in his arms, his fingers pressing the soft flesh against the bones painfully but it was the only way he could get a grip. He felt he was carrying a weight of darkness, he contained such a weight also, the least he could do was to carry hers. And the darkness in her body did not weigh much.

'I must do some shopping this afternoon,' she said, yawning. While he was drinking his tea she had been looking at four irregularly shaped spots on the side of his not very white jersey. They were dark, as though dust had adhered. They must have been jam. But William did not eat jam. Four of them.

'Did you find the cheese?'

'Yes thanks. It was rather good. We need bread.'

'I know. Thanks for doing the kitchen.'

'It looks rather smart doesn't it.'

She noticed he had put several things away in the wrong place.

'Did you read that bit in the paper?'

'Oh, I'm sorry. I forgot. Tell me about it.'

'Good God no! It was nothing. Can't think why I mentioned it. One has to talk about something. You've been a bit short on the chat side of late.'

He filled the kitchen with his demands! He was like an enormous monster between her and the air. She had nothing against him, or against his body. His pallor, the rather attractive sharpness of the way they had re-set his nose, his clear eyes – he was attractive to her. It was simply that he filled too large an area of her life. She did not want him out of her life, but the part of her that was not him was squashed, suffocating. Something in her squealed to be free, to get out from under this vast male life stalled above it, flattening it, eating it.

She had an idea it was part of being a woman, this sense of suffocation. She identified it with other feelings that had arrived at different times which she had noticed men did not share. For instance the involuntary detached warmth towards one's own children which almost immediately, with luck, became love. But the tenderness was impersonal, as though programmed, and for a time remained constant. There were other feelings she had had, often they coincided with rhythms of her own body but she was not able to write them off as merely physical because men did not have them. Her female psyche existed, fretted, gnashed, turned on itself and bit. Women are private too, she felt like shouting.

'Can I get you anything when I'm out?' Her voice sounded sharp, high-pitched in her own ears.

'I could do with some whisky,' said William, digging unhopefully into his pockets for some money.

Of course he didn't have any. He never had. Heaven knows what they would have done without her small savings. What a child he was! And yet she knew he wasn't. Oh enough of all this; if only she could get out. If he would only go and leave her space to find her coat and the car-key!

William was wondering why on earth he was still fond of this frightful shrew. Nothing she did seemed to make any difference. Perhaps it was just laziness. Maybe he just found it easier to be fond of people. Then he remembered all the people he could hardly bear to stay in the same room with. He never tired of Beryl. She lived in the darkness he could not find. Life with her could never be trivial, it tottered daily over the real abyss, every day of avoidance of toppling was a drama, and a triumph.

They collided at the door and Beryl drew in her breath. Then she squeezed his arm looking towards the door where the coats were. She let him go and went towards it, leaving him with that mixture of gratitude and resentment, resentment that he could feel grateful for such small crumbs from her, feeling put in his place, reduced, but happy at the curious passion that still joined them. She left him standing in the kitchen doorway, with no glance back and an unplanned slam of the front door; left an empty house and William, puzzled what to do for a moment, glad to remember he had potatoes to plant, clumping, a little self-consciously clumping and bumbling, true to the picture of himself she had left him with, to fetch the seed potatoes and his spade.

6

It made a noise like a bubble, an enclosing, liquid sound. 'Was that a hoopoe?' William was unable to see it clearly, enclosed as he was by dark leaves; a pigeon-sized bird.

'Didn't see it.' Edward half-lay, half-sat in the open on the hard soil of the hillside that looked green from a distance, but close-to the blades of grass were seen to be infrequent. William seemed unable to sit down, kept wandering off, which was a pity because he wanted to talk to him although, God knows, he had already done enough talking.

William had grown disproportionately older in the three years since they had last met. The process had taken place whereby the face that still contained the lineaments of the young man, frosted a little, furrowed with use, had turned in the other direction; instead of looking back to the original face of youth it now looked forward to – what? – to a death mask, to the skull. His face was nearer to the bones beneath it. There was a loss of colour too, Edward thought. Not that William ever had very much, the famous reconstruction had given him a pallor that hardly varied, and had left him almost wrinkle-free; not colour perhaps but a colourfulness was what his face and his body now lacked. As he clambered and peered among the trees, bird-watching glasses round his neck, in an open shirt and old drill trousers, he took a little longer to negotiate a bank, one arm hooked round a branch as he descended, as if loth to let go. When he did let go his legs were wooden, as though beneath his trousers were stilts in place of limbs. But he was the same; a little less patient perhaps, and disinclined to tease himself, though he teased Edward; but the same, despite the way his life seemed to have changed.

Edward lay flat and closed his eyes. There came into his mind a picture of another William he had seen at a public dinner. It was a fund-raising affair, for some piece of conservation that Edward had been passionately concerned with at the time and about which William had been characteristically evasive. But at Edward's entreaty he had agreed to be guest of honour and to speak.

For Edward it had been an evening filled with William-surprises. Not the least of them was his appearance; clean, brushed, in a dark suit and a thin white polo-necked sweater. Edward had never seen him away from the country and he looked slim, eager, even rather formidable. With the changed appearance there was a change of manner, he was quick – even smooth. People made much of him and he responded with the formal modesty of the star. A tamed William.

But the biggest surprise was the speech. It was very funny. It bore little relevance to the reason for the dinner, to the relief of most of the diners. Instead, William laid himself out to make them laugh. This he managed to do by using almost every device known to the professional comedian. At one point, having poised his glasses on his forehead the better to address his audience directly, by some imperceptible movement he caused them to slip back onto his nose at precisely the right moment in his anecdote leaving him blinking into an enormous roar of laughter. At the end, in another sort of gathering, the audience would have hoisted him on their shoulders, he was the hero of the evening; and he had said nothing. The opportunity had been there to say much about things presumably near his heart and he had not used it.

Edward asked him about this afterwards, feeling a prig but shocked despite himself, and William had answered shortly: 'I've written about it,' allowing himself to be swept off to another group where he continued to perform.

Edward felt more surprise than disapproval. He had not realized what a conscious choice of role the bumbling rural William represented. He could have been a lion, at least for a time. He had chosen not to be. For the first time Edward realized he had been unconsciously patronizing William, granting him the respect reserved for the saint at the edge of the world, a splendid fellow doubtless but because of his nature not subject to the choices and temptations of other mortals.

Yet part of his success could be attributed to the audience's relief. They had expected to be lectured by the rural saint and had instead found a buffoon eager to entertain them. How often could he have pulled it off?

Perhaps he did so all the time now, since he had moved back to London? Edward watched William clambering gingerly about the hillside. His jobs sounded dismal, chairman of a nature-lover's radio programme, and so on.

William squinted from shadow along the slope of the hill to where Edward sat in the open and was able to make him seem to be reclining on an unbroken cushion of flowers. By looking sideways along the slope he could give himself the impression there was nothing but these flowers. Two lines of the book of Job occurred to him: *Mischief does not grow out of the soil, nor trouble spring from the earth*. Edward lay on the earth, apparently packed with trouble. *Man is born to trouble as the sparks fly upward*.

He went back to join him. During the last few days he had been put in the absurd position of trying to explain to Edward why Edward should not take his own life. He could no longer think of any good reasons. The ones he had offered had sounded progressively more feeble. Now he merely sought to avoid interrogation. Edward made this difficult. William did not mind Edward using him in this fashion, he had simply run out of ideas. But there was no denying that the despair of Edward – if despair it was – had made the Tuscan landscape exceptionally vivid to him. His gloomy logic had made everything even more than usually interesting to William; everything, that is, except Edward.

He now sat next to him and Edward managed to convey by his immobility his opinion of the worthlessness, even the vulgarity, of William's bird-watching, botanizing, local-historicizing.

It was Edward, sighing now, smiling at him, shifting his position slightly, as though waiting for death to come, or for lunchtime, who had explained to William the history of the majestic hillfarms, all deserted, one of which they looked down on now. An hour before they had wandered through the cool proportioned rooms under those sunburned tiles. A perfect building, sharing the landscape as though it had been planted and had grown. Inside the high cool rooms the whitewashed walls looked dark around the windows so bright was the sky the windows framed. Signs of labour were still there, signs of leisure too. On the ground floor were wooden vats, presses, byres and above them, outside the living quarters, was a shaded verandah tiled in worn terracotta from which you could see, even though the house appeared to hug the earth, across the vine terraces, across the trees, to the tower of the church of the local town five miles away.

It had been deserted only for a few years. The long walls were covered with writing, done with a candle flame. There were lingams and yonis, carefully drawn, each with its one blind eye; there was a witty, obscene rhyme Edward translated for William, laughing. But mostly the writing in careful lines the length of the walls was a reasoned argument: that the land belonged to the people who worked it, that to be driven from here by high rents demanded by inheritors who lived as princes in the distant towns was a crime, the good sweat of generations wasted.

William wondered if the sexual drawings had been done by the same hand as the commonsense politics. He found himself hoping not; the rhyme in particular belonged to a lower order of sophistication. It stuck in his head:

Lo scrisse Dante
lo confermo Achille:
chi non lecca la fica
é un imbecile.

Well, doubtless they were complex people who had lived there, with different moods. But there was a purity in the building, in the passions expressed on the wall, in the landscape outside, so brilliantly organized, that was missing from the rhyme and the drawings. Not that the rhyme was 'impure', necessarily, in the Victorian sense of impurity, but the need to write it on the wall was. William hoped the generations who had lived in that house might have taken such things for granted, a part of life and pleasure. But had anyone, ever? Those one-eyed blind symbols haunted and hunted us all. It was William's turn to sigh.

Edward was talking about Helen: about how right she had been to leave him. William thought: he misses her, we both do, but he's probably telling the truth.

He said he'd been destroying her with his indecisiveness, his inability to make a go of the farm, with their chronic shortage of money which he seemed unable to solve.

William's knowledge of women – if he had any; the delicacy of his position with Edward, whose calm promise to make away with himself he tried to take seriously, had made William tread so slowly and carefully in his dealings with him that he had time to doubt whether he knew anything about anything – at any rate, what little he had observed of them led William to doubt that women like Helen leave men so suddenly and it seemed finally for those reasons. In William's view, that only happens when two events coincide: the woman becomes wholly convinced she is not loved, and she meets someone else who convinces her that she is, if not loved, at least seriously wanted. William pondered this with appreciation. He could find no flaw in such behaviour by women.

He turned his attention to Edward at his side. He was handsome, with his long nose and thin mouth; a strong face and a humorous one. He could have wished for a little more humour from him just now, for a little more – *outgoingness*. But that was to wish him to be somebody else. The effort to be fair tired him. At least it was a fact that just at the moment he would have found Edward's company extremely dispiriting if he had allowed himself.

Edward lay back with a bit of grass between his teeth, it moved as he spoke, his eyes shut against the glare. Nightingales sang fruitily around them, in daylight, which William had forgotten they did. One perched on top of a bush not ten yards away. A fat brown bird like a large sparrow, undeniably a nightingale, William got the glasses on it, because it began lustily to sing. He had never seen one before and at his quiet exclamation Edward obediently sat up, slowly so as not to startle it, and took the glasses, returning them after raising them briefly to his eyes.

It really was bad luck, to be in a paradise with such a companion! Admittedly a paradise from which Adam and Eve had been driven and in which they were merely spectators.

But a paradise. Neglect, at these Italian altitudes, brought nothing rank with it, except perhaps trailing briars. The place was probably more sweet and colourful in its wildness than it had ever been, or ever would be again. Nature had not yet won it back entirely, though it was true he had just skirted, as it lay sleeping, the largest snake he had seen outside a zoo. But that would have been there anyway.

Over the vines which trailed from their sagging poles along the ground, sometimes for twenty feet or more, grew swathes of honeysuckle, mostly with rose-cream flowers, but some were clouds of butter-yellow.

In the middle distance between themselves and the house, supported presumably on an old vine-pole, but looking as though it began and ended in air, was a corona of pink dogroses. The shadowy trees buzzed with invisible nectar-sucking flies which did not bother them but which sometimes caught the light and flashed gold.

'What makes you contented with so little?' said Edward.

In the midst of his enjoyment William was exasperated. 'Whatever makes you demand too much, and the wrong things?'

Edward continued to smile, eyes closed. 'Some of the greatest men have been great because of the outrageousness of their demands.'

William, thinking of the first notoriously discontented man who came into his head whom he also admired, said: 'Baudelaire always gives the impression, in his letters anyway, that he'd be happy if only he could get hold of his inheritance.'

'Anyway – I'm not a great man. Far from it. Useless at everything,' said Edward.

He was perhaps not much of a farmer. 'Your films? Your

painting?' said William, politely. Of all the causes for self-dissatisfaction the one he had least respect for was doubt about personal gifts. As though it mattered whether a man was gifted or not! This exaltation of the 'creative'. He had known men who moaned through life because they weren't good novelists, or painters. Who cares? There are too many writers and painters anyway. Life, difficult enough God knows, is more important than the expression of it!

He fastened his attention on some poplars growing next to the house. The breeze bent them to the east, dark on that side, bright on the other, their branches a series of plateaux of bright and dark green. Between the poplars and where they sat were four wide-grown willows, another shade of green, greeny-grey, and the wind treated them differently, taking them from below, blowing them upwards like green fountains in slow-motion. Between him and the willows were yellow-flowered grasses, and between his knees was a tiny closed flower, its head the colour of ripe strawberries and the size of the head of a match.

' ... dabbling,' finished Edward. He opened his eyes and watched William fish an apple from his pocket and take a bite. 'Shall we go back to lunch?' he said politely, raising himself on his elbow. 'No,' said William, 'let's stay here.'

He stretched himself out again. He was certainly putting old William through it. But perhaps he could get him to say the one surprising thing that would break through the envelope of indifference that seemed to have grown round him. So, presumably, he wanted to be rescued? Nevertheless he suspected that the nothingness which he found in the world around him was nearer to the truth than William's evasions. He looked at William's brown wrist terminating in the surprising white of the back of his bent, claw-like hand as he ate the apple. There was something elegant about the wrist and the muscled arm, with the shirtsleeve rolled carefully to just below the elbow, and the way William's clean profile picked cleanly into the apple which he held steady in front of his face, gazing across it to the trees around the house. Surely no one had ever been smashed up and put together so well.

'You're like other people,' said Edward. 'A bit of

affection here, a bite of an apple there, a nice view. You had a second chance. Being remade. Odd it should make you *more* like other people than most are like other people – and the second time round.'

'You don't know what I was like before.'

'What were you like?'

'Just the same I think.'

'So it made no difference? That seems a waste.'

William addressed the strawberry flower in front of him. 'I suppose it does. When it was touch and go, when there were chances I might snuff it, ordinary things like weather – especially weather – became rather enviable. Important.' William paused. 'Very,' he added, as though an afterthought, taking a last bite from his apple, putting the core beside him on the earth and looking at his watch.

'You want to go?' said Edward.

'No, not at all.'

'Apples. What about people?'

'No more important than the weather. But the weather was very important. Thirty-one seconds.'

'What?'

'Before the ants found the applecore.'

'William you are *avoiding* me!'

'Of course.'

'I want some eloquent defence of life that makes me take up my bed and walk.'

'Why does it have to be surprising?'

'Apples and weather?'

'Yes.'

'Well, I've got some sort of admission out of you I suppose. It's like squeezing an old toothpaste tube. You only let out enough to cover a toothbrush.'

William stared across at the house. 'They were extraordinarily selfish and shortsighted, the landlords, to drive the farmers away from here.'

'We all are. You agree with that stuff on the wall?'

'Absolutely.'

'The child of one of those greedy landlords might be a great poet in Rome. With nothing to do but write – and watch the weather.' Edward granted William a respectful smile after he said this.

William had only recently become the recipient of such smiles, half-teasing, half-deferential, from those younger than himself. At first they had puzzled him, then he realized they were aimed at a person he did not know he had yet become: an old man, past it.

He grinned, he hoped boyishly, tossing the smile back. 'I watch the weather, yes.' I've never really been a man at all, he thought. I've stayed a child in a garden, or tried to. Edward has struggled with the world, that's good, even if the result at the moment is a litter of abandoned vehicles outside the farm, and inside the farm a pile of washing-up and emptiness.

'You could be lying here instead of me,' said Edward.

'Easily.'

'So my fellow-prisoner's staying mum. But suppose you were in my position, and you were asking these boring questions, what do you think would be the most helpful thing I could say to you?'

'Let's go home and do the washing-up.'

'You do know, don't you, that one can get into a frame of mind when commonsense isn't enough.'

'Yes I do know.'

William thought of Beryl. He had not liked leaving her in that place. But she would be well looked after, she'd even seemed to like it the last time, and it was only for a few days. But oddly enough, of all the things he feared for Beryl he could not imagine her even playing with the idea of taking her own life. She was, he thought, with a surge of warmth for her, insufficiently self-involved. He wanted to go back to her. He wasn't doing much good here. But Edward, on the simplest level, must be lonely. It was strange he planned to take them both to a distant party tonight. If he was in the frame of mind he said he was what possible interest could there be in a party? Still, perhaps some company was better than none.

The sun was up higher now and it was a long hot walk, even in the shade of the tangled chestnuts that covered the slopes of the hills. The track was rough and badly rutted by foresters' tractors and William's ankles kept going over. He regretted his heavy boots which he had left in England because he had thought them unsuitable for Italy.

They came out into the open and began the climb down, past more abandoned farms, to where Edward lived. They pushed through banks of thin flowers, mostly yellow and white, and William made Edward repeat the names of the extraordinary variety of delicate multi-leaved grasses that grew thinly, separately, everywhere: erba medica, lucerne, lupanella. There were yellow whins, more honeysuckle, flowers among the grasses like kingcups only white with an orange centre, and dandelions a pale canary yellow. As they disturbed them among the flowers and grasses small blue butterflies rose unhurriedly and resettled.

The last part of their walk was along a dust road and at a bend by the roadside was a cross. The boy killed there by the German soldiers had been fourteen; he had been caught taking food to the partisans at night. In the village behind them chickens picked about in the dust in front of the houses, a dog barked, a woman came out clanking a bucket, calling to Edward, she had some eggs for him. He went towards her and William stood looking at the cross. It was easy to imagine: the excited boy leaving his mother in the dark, looking forward to being welcomed and slapped on the back by his heroes, the approaching noise of engines, hiding, headlights, trucks stopping, engines still turning, the challenge, the chase, the stumble, the rough hands, looking up for the faces of his captors blinded by their torches, cowering, not believing it, whimpering, the pistol shot, or the short burst of automatic fire... The soldiers talking, climbing into their vehicles, driving into the village, searching – it seemed fruitlessly, there was only one cross – driving on. Silence.

There was something important buried not very deep below the pictures that had crowded into him as he stood there in the darkness of thirty years ago. He saw it again: it was the boy's face in the torchlight. Everything else was absurd: the man-invented engines, the man-invented men with their orders and their guns (perhaps some of their friends had been shot by the partisans), it was all machine-like and forgivable. Only one thing was not absurd: the life that was in the boy; and the deprivation of it ...

He came to himself on the sunlit road, Edward approaching him gingerly carrying a small parcel of eggs wrapped in newspaper, with a thought in his head that he saw was obvious as soon as it became a thought and ceased to be a picture, and it faded quicker than a picked wild flower. But he trusted feelings, pictures, and the picture of the face of the boy, the sense of the hands clutching his arm, had turned his blood cold and had vitalized him, assured him again of the value of life because something so seen, so felt, was too powerful to be denied.

This must be what Edward had lost.

He wanted to hurry to show him the flower that had bloomed again in his mind; it was already wilting, fading in the hot sunlight on the dusty road with the cross at the side of it, brief writing in the centre. He felt dumb, as though a weight had clamped itself round his tongue.

He said a brief prayer for the soul of the boy. He had never been able quite to believe that prayers for somebody or something could be efficacious: statements of opinion merely, like writing a letter to *The Times* – which brought us back to the absurd. But oh the flower, the flower that had bloomed! They left the road and brushed through grasses again, walked through the flocks of blue butterflies, Edward carefully carrying the eggs in front of him, one hand underneath, the other on top, like a priest with a chalice.

Perhaps he did not see grasses, butterflies, crosses, or hear nightingales that sang now, again, in the thin woods on the approach to the house.

They picked their way through the abandoned carcasses of lorries, tractors, cars that somehow Edward had brought down there at their last gasp and never been able to mend, or never tried. Tyres, rusty pieces of machinery, and also enormous bones, littered the outside of the house. The bones puzzled William, presumably they were the debris of horses but where or why had Edward got those? Perhaps he had arranged the outside of his house as a picture of the inside of his mind: a historical mess, reaching back into the past; footprints of dinosaurs, in the bone-dry earth around the olive trees, and rock-like dinosaur turds the size of sofas.

Death can enter a man before he dies. That was a mystery, worthy of prayer; William could think of no other way of trying to unlock it, though he had no great faith in prayer, except as a solace to himself. Perhaps a grace would enter Edward; something to make his demands less grandiose – or rather, more, much more, grandiose, because there was grandeur in the day that surrounded them which, it was possible, Edward could no longer see. William did not blame him, for Edward might have travelled to places William had not dreamed of and they might be finally chilling.

A neighbouring family was cutting Edward's green hay. They had the hands he lacked. In return they took a proportion of the crop. Their old red tractor was pulling away a high load, already slightly browning in the sun. William caught its fragrance. It was kept from toppling by a pile of brown children who sat on top, staring. The man on the tractor waved at Edward who waved back. Three women, sun-bleached cloths over their heads, carried on raking cut hay into swathes, one of them bent almost parallel to the ground she was so old. They had been at it since dawn, William had heard them arrive when he was in bed. He had got up and looked out. There were still white balls of mist in the clefts of the tree-covered hills around them. The day had dawned unbelievably new and fresh and their voices were quiet and slow as though they were still attached to sleep, almost as though their work was a part of it. There was no bustle, only a slow bending to the task before them, in the dew, and surrounded by the soft white bales of vapour on the hills which were like the earth's sleep.

Inside the house the kitchen was dark and the flies were noisy above the dirty plates and the lidless swill bucket. Edward poured them both some young wine he had made himself, for his trailing vines still delivered enough sad-looking grapes to make that possible. William drank greedily, it was bitter and clean; he poured himself another tumbler of it while waiting for the water to run hot from the

tap at the sink. It did not because the geyser was broken.
'Didn't you know?'
'Edward. Don't you think if you made yourself more comfortable you might cheer up?'
'Geysers break.'
'Can be mended.'
'Guttoso was meant to come last week.'
'Shall we chase him up?'
'You can't chase Guttoso. Anyway, he just lost two fingers at the sawmill.'

William had heard himself sound like Beryl at her worst. Edward stood impassive, outwardly humble, waiting for what William next had to say, the house and farm were so obviously a shambles. William knew there was something aggressive in his attitude of submission, even something splendid, for he was saying, by the carefully sad expression on his face, by the slightly stooped angle of his body: 'Say on, say on, and all you say is true. But if you'd stop bustling round like Martha and use your intelligence instead of your complacence you'd see it doesn't matter and you'd laugh.'

So William laughed and they both filled a huge saucepan with water and put it on the stove to warm up. The gas came from a *bombola* and William immediately suspected it was going to run out. He kicked it, to see if it gave out a reassuringly full sound; it did not, it rang, and Edward looked at it.

Suddenly he clenched his jaw fiercely and rushed at it, bent, seized it in both arms, lifted it and shook it. 'We can pick up some this afternoon,' he said, between gritted teeth. Meanwhile there seemed enough gas to take the chill off the water for the washing-up and they both sat down to wait at the long table, the flask of wine between them. William filled both their glasses and raised his to the still scowling Edward. Whereupon, to William's great delight, Edward gave one of the enormous grins he remembered from years ago, threw back his head and laughed with a huge shout, righted his chair, settled his elbows on the table and raised his glass to William. There was some hard Parmesan cheese on a piece of paper on the table, much visited by flies, and they nibbled at that, drinking. The fare is just about the same as at home, thought William, emptying his glass and refilling it, but this is fun.

The black dog bothered him. A skinny beast which fastened adoring eyes on his master hoping to be fed. This, as far as William could see, it never was. As usual Edward took no notice. After a while the dog went to rummage in the swill pail, turning it over, Edward shouted in Italian and the dog scurried away to a corner, twisting its hindquarters away from danger. William resisted the need to right the swill bucket and replace its contents.

In a corner was a mothy dog on wheels; a pile of children's records, out of their sleeves, was by the battery gramophone, a glass on top of them inside which old wine had dried leaving a dark scab, and still pinned to the wall was a child's drawing of a lop-sided house. William could see no trace left behind by Helen, unless it was the rather pretty plates they were soon to wash up, but Edward was fond of such things too. They had talked briefly of Helen when William had first arrived but Edward had discouraged questions. He obviously regarded the sweep as clean and beyond argument. Perhaps he wanted it to be.

The sounds of haymaking floated into the dark kitchen. William had an impulse to go outside to the brightness; perhaps Edward was only staying in to keep him company? No, Edward shook his head. 'They have their own methods.' The saucepan of water was now giving off a little steam so they put their glasses on what room they could find on the draining board, set the *fiasco* of wine between them on the floor and Edward rolled up his sleeves. William scraped their yesterday's plates and – it took harder scraping – their day-before-yesterday's into the swill bucket which he put right way up before he did so. There! William felt happily justified. A time for everything! He was rather drunk and quite under the sway of Edward; delighted with him.

They were half-way through their task, noisily splashing and clanking, when there came an imperious, metallic rap on the door, quickly repeated, hard. They stopped; it was an unfriendly, dangerous sound. Edward, his arms held over the basin, flecked with detergent bubbles, stared down for a moment, abstracted, and then, still holding his dripping arms bent and away from his sides, went to open half the double door that led directly from the outside into the kitchen. The dog followed him. An oblong of extreme brightness dazzled William, peering to see who it was, and it seemed to be a man in uniform, in belt and buckles and a peaked hat, with his arm raised threateningly. Edward stood at the door, drying his arms with his handkerchief, neither going out to the top of the steps to join the policeman nor inviting him in. Something glinted in his hand and William saw it was a key, he had been rapping on the door with the point of his car-key, which taken with the crispness of his uniform was a curiously confident and aggressive gesture. He went to join Edward at the door and the *carabiniere* turned towards him. 'Your friend?' William understood Edward to say something like, 'I don't usually have my enemies to stay' and felt nervous about this cheeking of authority. The man looked at William as though memorizing his face, and grunted. Then he looked down at the dog. 'It ought to be tied up.' 'It never leaves the house,' said Edward, untruthfully. The policeman smiled, leaving a silence. 'There is a law. I could have you out of the country.' 'So you have said.' 'May I see your wife?' 'She is not here.' The man smiled again, as if it was what he had expected. 'If she was your wife.' William felt Edward relax at this. 'Would you repeat that?' he said. The smile went from the policeman's face and they stared at each other. 'You won't forget tomorrow, will you?' he said. 'Just a formality. I would like to see your permit.' 'You have already seen it.' 'There are one or two details. Two o'clock?' 'Two o'clock.' He stood, attempting to outstare Edward, then turned and ran down the steps swinging his key from its leather tag like a propeller. He paused at the bottom to look slowly along the line of debris, making sure they saw him look, got back into his white car without looking round and roared off up the hill spurting gravel from his back wheels.

William was shaken. He disliked the mess himself but he had forgotten the hatred that lies inside a limited sense of order, the speed and cruelty with which it will pounce on difference if it also suspects weakness. He had led a protected life in England.

Edward appeared to have enjoyed himself. He was especially pleased at the 'if she was your wife' remark. He reckoned the policeman had played into his hands. He was new here, from the South, and particularly hated foreigners, with good reason regarding them as a source of trouble and immorality.

'There's been a drug scene in the English colony. It's O.K. My papers are in order. He just thinks I'm poor and undesirable. I am. And I don't care what he thinks.' Edward shrugged. He seemed secure, whereas the visit had awakened insecurities in William he had not known he possessed. He wanted a siesta. Moving away from Edward, his hand on the handle of the door to the passage that led to his room he said: 'These are bad times.'

'Worse than other bad times?' Edward was back at the sink. Having embarked on the washing-up he did it with obsessive care.

'There are only two faiths. In God or in Man. We've lost both.'

'Most of us never had much reason to believe in either.'

'You have to pretend a bit,' said William, 'just to keep things going. Otherwise what's to stop the policeman shooting us if he felt like it.'

'That happens in places.'

William nodded, abstracted. 'I believe in grace and you don't.'

'The kind that suddenly arrives from sources unknown? No.'

'You should. Otherwise there's no hope.'

Edward was drying his hands on a very grey towel. 'You're gloomier than I am.'

'Oh yes. I'm going to have a rest.'

'Flights of angels attend thee.'

William managed a gloomy laugh and after he had shut the door from the kitchen behind him found himself entirely in the dark. It was a part of the farm not used now that Helen and the children were gone, the shutters onto the courtyard were never opened. His room was at the end and at last, after bending double over an unexpected chest and bruising his cheek on an empty candlestick, he found himself in the comparative light of his shady room, his shutters on a loose latch, a crack of light between them. He did not look out but knelt at the side of his bed his face in his hands, smelling the dusty bedcover. He had drunk too much and was headachy, but it was this relentless questioning of even the necessity of life by Edward that bore him down, entered him, made him feel desperate; his confidence was fragile. Of course. It would have been a great relief to him, overstrained, if he could have cried. He envied women their easy access to tears. They were not a measure of the importance of a feeling but they were a great help.

He took off his shoes and lay on the bed, wishing he could snooze as easily as he had when younger. He reached for a book in the little shelf below his bedside-table, his hovering fingers settling on a paperback in the familiar green covers – the Olympia Press, was it? – of the French pornography of his youth. He was not disappointed. It turned out to be *L'histoire d'O*, a well-written fantasy of female degradation, sexual slavery. It was cruel, and ingenious in its inventiveness. Yes, he contained such things. He tried to imagine himself doing them and failed. But what a slender skin of convention and education kept such things and mankind apart! A skin that had broken once in his lifetime. We would never live down the horrors of those camps. But what if the skin should break, for us all ...?

With a gasp of distress he put the book aside and rolled off the bed, stumbling to the window, opening the shutters. Hardly more light came into the room because the sun was on the other side of the house, but from shadow he looked out through the leaves of a climbing fig tree (Edward had warned him to keep his shutters closed because poisonous snakes sometimes climbed it) onto the bright green meadow. The birds were silent now in the full heat of the day. The stripes where the hay had just been cut were freshly and wetly green, the long stalks had preserved the dew. The part of the field cut only an hour before was a lighter colour and the women of the family, quiet again, like the birds, bent in a line, their heads enclosed in the sun-whitened cloths, tidying and turning the green hay. It never failed. His heart rose. *Nothing* could prevent the outside world helping us, if we let it. It stayed outside man's dark head, whatever he did to it, and saved him. Or it could.

He got out his notebook and sat in a chair; from where he sat he could no longer see the haymaking, only the sky. 'A hoopoe. A liquid sound, like a bubble,' he wrote. Their morning was gone from him, empty, like the farmhouse, hollow; a bubble ... He came to himself, his head in a hard angle of the chair-back, an unpleasant taste of stale wine between his teeth. 'A little strawberry-coloured flower,' he wrote, and gazed up at the sky; burning gold it was, only by an effort of memory could you see it was blue; cloudless, featureless, burning.

He woke again, later, to remember he had dreamed briefly of chains, wrist-fetters, like the ones fitted to Laurence Olivier in the film of *The Beggar's Opera*. Fetters you could sing in – even if not very well. That was the influence of *L'histoire d'O*. But his wrists and his faceless partner's wrists had been coated with Vaseline, the fetters slipped off smoothly. He remembered the touch of his fingers on his partner's dry palm. He remembered who she was – a girl of long ago he had not thought of for years – but the chief memory was one of touch, the brush of the tips of his fingers on her palm. Such a small thing and in his dream, and now, endlessly significant.

Why do we make such enormous demands? Our imagination makes demands but life contradicts them. We do not need the strong tastes our imaginations pretend to crave. We do not need chains, tortures, subjugations. We can select and imagination is content: stirs sometimes, bubbles nastily; can be allowed to do so. We can admit our imaginings, but they are ours, we are not theirs. We can still choose. There is no need to go whoring after despair. Like Edward.

He got up from the chair stiffly, chilled. He went to a drawer and pulled it open, looking for his sweater. It was the only thing there and as he held it out to pull it over his head a headline stared up at him from the newspaper lining the drawer. HAPPINESS A SNARE WHEN THE WORLD IS A HORRIBLE PLACE. Incredulous, he bent down and saw it was a quotation from an interview with Simone de Beauvoir. Nearly all his life, it seemed to him, people like Simone de Beauvoir had been saying things as contrary to commonsense as that. These *were* bad times; at no other time could anyone advance so confidently an idea so self-evidently false. Was it *happiness* that brought about the horrors of the world! William snorted indignantly as he pulled the sweater over his head. Did happy men become torturers? Was there, he demanded from a cloud of wool, such a thing as a *happy* secret policeman? Complacence was bad, yes (but not, William sighed, all *that* bad; some of us could do with a little more) but *happiness*! He went to the window and stared out, seeing nothing because he was so indignant. The greatest gift one man could give to another was the emanation of his happiness. What did the confounded woman mean by the word? – he went back to the drawer and twisted his head sideways. To his annoyance, because he felt his indignation had been wasted, he noticed, although it was in a way distasteful to him, that she sounded both happy *and* complacent. What she said was simply that although happy herself happiness was a snare 'if you thought the world was a happy place.' In other words the idiot said nothing! William was unable to imagine a single human being who had ever entertained such a thought for longer, say, than a blissful five minutes. And for this young lovers must dutifully warn one another in the midst of their blisses, and old buffers like himself, rapt by the beauty of haymaking, must remember that the sweat is not on *their* brows. The joyless puritanisms of the time. Even *L'histoire d'O* was puritanism – a natural shame monstrously, vengefully projected.

He felt the need to define happiness but rejected it because, after all, de Beauvoir hadn't bothered and she'd already wasted enough of his time. What he had in mind was the animal response of one's life to the life of the world around it, a source of understanding, a grace – that word which had fallen between him and Edward with a dull clunk, like a plastic saucer. He could almost see it still lying there on the dirty floor of the kitchen, himself too proud to pick it up; Edward regarding it, like so much else on the floor, as something to be stepped over.

He was restless now. He wondered if siesta time was over. He could do with another drink, once you started drinking it was essential to keep it up. He had heard Edward go out earlier, presumably to give a hand with the hay. Then he had come back. Perhaps he was only beginning his siesta now, when William wanted company. Irritating.

In fact Edward was in his room painting. He had come in from the hay-making because he had felt, as usual, spare. The Orissis were a self-contained unit, with their own rhythms and they treated him with friendly politeness, as though he were a sort of squireen – for after all it was his hay. This he would have disliked anyway, the sense of being an exploiter it would have given him; but in this case he had the additional irritation of knowing that far from his exploiting them, they were exploiting him. There was no way of exactly measuring what proportion of the crop was theirs. Edward knew, and they knew he knew, that prudence demanded they weighed the scales heavily in their favour. After all, would not the crop have been wasted if they had not cut it for him? So for the sake of his temper, and his *figura*, it was better he kept out of the way. He would have liked to run the whole place himself, restore the overgrown land to what it had once been, the envy of the neighbourhood. Old men still spoke with wonder of the cherry-harvest there; in their youth they had made a little festival of it, and the olive crop was nearly as good still. But he was tied by lack of money.

He would probably have made a mess of it anyway.

Besides, the farm was Helen's.

"His" hay was really Helen's hay, was Orissi's hay stored away in barns to feed another man's cattle.

He was an irrelevance and had a real relationship with nothing. The fields and terraces he worked were like a stomach, digesting him, ejecting him. He was the least important event in their long history. He would be forgotten the moment he drove up the long track for the last time and looked down at the beautiful, simple house, to catch it settling back, immediately, into the long patience of its own affairs.

... A foreigner lived there once, with his wife. Their children ran wild and were allowed to get their clothes dirty. We liked her, she was *simpatica*. He was a strange fellow, difficult to tell whether he was a *signore* or not, he too dressed dirtily. Their marriage finished. This is usually what happens to the marriages of foreign people who come here. She went away. They did not live here long. He? Well, he ...

Edward paused with his brush in the air and stopped dramatizing himself. He had no idea whether he had the courage – or the energy – to put an end to a life he had a settled conviction was pointless: nor any idea how he would set about such a thing if he so decided. What he was waiting for, and it seemed to him time was running out and to wait any longer would be a postponement and a failure, was something inside himself or outside himself that would help him make up his mind.

It was not that he had made a cock of farming that he minded so much, or, before that, of film-making. At film-making, he reminded himself, it was not strictly true that he had failed. There had been aspects of the work that he enjoyed and had therefore been good at. He had been good at finding the bones of a subject and at photographing these so they held together and made sense. He enjoyed the feeling of security it gave him when he knew in his head that the bones held. He had also enjoyed cutting his films, knowing, or feeling he knew, precisely the moment to press the button on the Movieola that stopped the film running and finding he was able to tell the editor precisely the frames that were to be joined. It was like being a conductor, you sang to yourself as the film flowed on, drawing it all together. There were even wonderful moments when some sequence in the earlier part of the film worried you, you snagged on it, then suddenly you saw why you had filmed it that way, realized that all those weeks ago on location, juggling the film, the filmcrew, the weather, the cash, you'd already seen the film as a whole, that piece fitted in perfectly somewhere else; you'd known, even unconsciously, exactly what you were doing.

Those were marvellous days, when you came out of the cutting-room your coat slung round your shoulders like a cloak; it seemed you greeted people who passed you in the corridor, and they greeted you, with new respect and freedom. In the canteen you stretched your legs under the table, tired, and thought: Yes, I am a director. That film works.

These were powerful satisfactions.

He stared, frowning, at his picture. It was a small landscape that he painted inside a frame, as though he wanted it to be finished even while he was painting it.

No, what had gone wrong with the filming was what was wrong with him. He had simply lost interest. He had stood outside, or above, or wherever it was he stood when he removed himself, and could see no point in going on. It amazed him that his colleagues could go on bustling round, making out worksheets, answering telephones, talking repetitively about the last job, looking forward sceptically to the next, and apparently content to go on doing this for the rest of their lives. Content enough. It was their job, it brought in the bread. It brought in his. He did not feel in any sense superior to them, as far as he could judge. It merely baffled him that they did not seem to see time as he did, draining away, and that all of them, give or take a satisfaction here and there, were simply marking time until they died. What else was there? All he knew was: there had to be something.

He had been able to leave because Helen had this farm. But they could have left too. Only a couple of years of saving would have got them off the treadmill. They did not want to get off.

He had been drawn to William because he did not need bustle to keep him going: appeared to be self-contented. When he had gone down to film him (he at first had made a great show of reluctance to have his peace invaded, probably genuine, but he became more and more fascinated by the processes of film-making and by the end was managing to write himself into every shot) he had been greatly impressed, and moved, to find it was possible to live as he did, as though time was a storm and he was in the eye of it. He had no distractions. There was no one he could chat to about the last job and no new job to plan. No jokes, no comradeship: an almost complete lack of outward event. He wrote, it was true, but his output was small. He had a wife also but there was not much of his life he appeared to share with her. No, he was on his tod, and perfectly happy.

Yet that film had been the beginning of the end for Edward. Because he had found – too early in his filming career – that there was something film could not express. He had felt a depth of peacefulness in William, a proper reaction, at last, to this terrible drifting away of days. They drifted away from William too, of course, but he let a day lie on his hand like powder, each grain inspected before night took it, and it was as though he blew the grains off his hand himself, standing outside his house at nightfall, without regret for they'd been acknowledged, thanked and now, like Ariel, could be set free.

He returned to the studio with his film, triumphant. He had made a friend, and the friend was Prospero. But when he put together the rough-cut he was appalled. It was a film of an elderly eccentric: vain, endearing, enthusing over ragged bushes, sparse trees – these came across quite well, but he did not – as though he owned them. The enthusiasm which communicated itself in the open and which William clearly and unselfishly wanted to share was, in the film, mildly potty. And his musings over stone walls were ridiculous.

In the dark of the viewing theatre someone had laughed.

When the lights went up he was congratulated, asked where he had found such a survival, and so funny. He was congratulated by men who were not glib fools but who had seen what he had seen on the film, a travesty. He should never have allowed it to be shown, but he did. It was in its way a good film, as truthful as he could make it, and the truth in the film was that William had nothing relevant to say.

That was a kind of truth.

Painting was better. A machine is too logical. He considered the masses of the willows in the left foreground, their movement was contrary to the movement of the poplars. It was there, he had done it quite well. Helen's figure to the right, small and brown, gave scale but was perhaps too carefully toned with the orange, nearly invisible, roof of the deserted farmhouse. The figure worried him but he still felt he needed it there.

It had been the same with Helen; the same process. The film had revealed a William that was at least partly true which obscured his early, thrilling, image of William forever. As time passed, with Helen, he did not only see her differently; it was much worse than that.

As he had lost interest in filming now he lost interest in women. Completely and horribly.

There had been a mystery and an excitement surrounding women, they were softer-skinned creatures from whom something could be learned. He came to see Helen as no different from himself, and therefore dreadful. He imagined her with her hair cut as short as his and her chest flattened. She wore his clothes anyway: a man with a fat bottom. Making love to her was a farce, it was sheer chance they had different organs. It was nonsense that he turned to her for solace, she to him for protection. Neither could provide either.

The children were dreams, slowly disintegrating: greedy, violent, deceitful. Their moments of beauty became daily more rare. Soon they would be awkward sulky versions of their parents, longing to be off, to start the whole process again. It was true what he saw. He knew it was ludicrously gloomy, but it was true.

Though still filled with sexual need he had ceased to desire Helen – how could he, she was no different from himself! – or any other women, or any man. He did not know what to do with his sexuality, it was a torture to him.

He painted out her figure quickly; immediately the picture looked better, delivered its intention more simply: a desolate green scene.

So that was the position he had arrived at ... It might be

bad or mad but that was how he was and what reason could there be to continue? He heard William pottering discreetly in the kitchen. If he saw the point of living he should be able to explain it. If he could not, let him admit the right of others to see it differently.

He put down his brush and looked at the picture. The trees were right. The house appeared to be drooping through them into a hole. The action of the wind was right, it was as though there was a storm, it was like a storm at sea, the trees green water, but it was taking place in a calm. There was calm in the picture and yet it was inside a storm, or a storm was inside it. William knocked.

Edward wanted to turn his picture so William could not see it but stopped himself. He had to let him in, he liked William, he wanted to remain friends with him, but he did not want him to say a word about his picture.

William stood outside the door determined to get in. He wanted to see the kind of picture Edward painted and he knew he would never be shown. He had thought of creeping into Edward's room and rummaging but an opportunity had not presented itself. The direct approach was better. He wondered if the delay was because he was hiding his paintings away but there was no sound of that sort of movement. Then came Edward's voice, so he opened the door and, pretending to be tentative, hovered on the threshold.

Edward said hello and turned his back to clean his brushes, putting them carefully away. 'I hope I'm not disturbing you?' 'No, I was just finishing.' From the door William could not see the picture he had obviously been working on, but he was surprised at its smallness and to see it was already framed. Stepping into the room, craning slightly – uninvited he could not stand squarely in front of it – he half-expected an incompetent horror-scene and saw instead a literal account of the place they had been that morning. He had thought Edward had not even looked at it. He also saw, with a touch of fear, that it was very good. He realised he would dislike it if Edward turned out to be a good artist.

The poplars and willows were right, he'd caught their counter-movement; the house was right too, the way it sank in amongst them as though on an air-filled cushion. William felt fear for another reason now, looking at the picture: because it was true and because it left out everything he had felt about the scene. There was light in it but it was a hostile stare; there was softness in it too but it crept out to suffocate.

At the side was a figure painted over, transparent, and it was right this should happen to any human presence on the scene, ingested, by the inexorable onward march of the staring greens. It was a masterpiece; horrible. It was horrible it should be already framed, as though Edward felt it might spread out of the canvas and eat him up. Or, more likely, the frame was exclusive, a defence against any other kind of meaning entering; it was a casing for the charge – the picture was a bullet aimed at his own head.

He had moved away from his neat box of brushes and was standing at the window with his back to William. It was clear he wanted no remark passed on his painting and William felt that whatever he said next he was going to be judged by. He did not care much, now, what the judgement would be. Because an attitude to life so determined was not to be cajoled. There was clearly no question of cheering Edward up – he was too formidable. Nevertheless, a question lay uppermost in his mind.

'Edward, who is that picture for?' He felt calm suddenly, as though all had been silliness between them before and this was the nakedness of the matter.

'For myself,' said Edward, turning, also suddenly relaxed.

'Why do you want to bring yourself such bad news if you already know it?'

'Why does one do anything?'

'Why not sleep?'

Edward shrugged. 'Energy has to be used up.'

'You know there's no hope in the picture. Energy to express hopelessness? Where does it come from?'

'You would just lie down?'

'I think so.'

'All right then – vanity. A desire to assert my wonderful temperament – as you assert yours.' He smiled at William. 'Why should God have all the good tunes?'

Why indeed, if that was still the case, which William doubted. But the joke for some reason reminded him of Dr Johnson and of a world of heartiness and commonsense and jokes that lived in sight of the abyss and attempted to defy it with these things. Had not Johnson himself, that helpless melancholic laugher, causer of laughter in others, once said: 'I may be cracking my joke and cursing the sun. Sun how I hate thy beams!'

Sun how I hate thy beams! William too, as he now rather proudly reminded himself, had known what it was to feel so. But Johnson did not savour his desolation and regard it as a revelation. He fought it with the weapons he had: friendship, work, drink. That was manly, that was true. Both were true, the manly defiance, and the dark defied. The relish of darkness was unmanly.

These were bad times because they made a cult of their

badness as though the dreadfulness of life was a modern discovery – like penicillin.

Edward could stand there smiling gently at him all he liked. He was caught in a modish trap. He denied the ordinary meat and two veg of life!

William hated the dark house, the absence of people, children, laughter, quarrels – forgetting for a moment the absence of most of these things in his own. He hated the skinniness of the cringing dog. *Of course* policemen rapped on the door with keys. Hostility is invited when all is seen as hostile.

'Of course it's hostile! Whoever thought otherwise!'

'What?'

William turned and went back to the kitchen. He poured himself a glass of wine at the sink, relishing the reminders of good fellowship the action gave him. Edward followed him out and stood, uncertain.

'I would rather vaporize about the prettiness of the willows than draw them over me like steel netting!'

'William – I've made you angry!'

'What else do you expect, painting a picture like that? You either mean it or you don't and if you mean it you've scared me to death! Have a drink.'

'I will.'

This was no world! William looked round the dark kitchen: everyone, everything, driven out of it except that dreadful dog. 'I've just been remembering there's a world outside. Couldn't we have some company?'

'Good idea.' Edward was placating, amused. 'We're going to Chiavelli tonight.'

'If the car will start!'

'Your car has been known not to start – your generator to run out of fuel.'

'Yes' he said, penitently. 'But – I don't think I can face the dark like you do. I think I'll go and wash. I don't feel too bright.'

'I'm afraid there's no water.'

'Eh?'

'We used the last for the washing-up.'

William began to laugh; no food, no fuel, no water. 'Till

when?'

'It's been pretty dry recently. Unless it's a stone in the pipe.'

'What do we do then?'

'We could go and look,' said Edward, vaguely.

William had been giggling but told himself to stop. Fuel did run out if it had to be transported from the nearest town, and food became short if you had little money. Water was hard to come by in these hills and there was nothing funny in not being attached to the mains. He was getting soft, he hadn't had to think about water for years. As a matter of fact it was time he got out of here and stopped having to think, he'd done enough for the time being and this kitchen was taking on the feel of an interrogation cell; we can't go on with the same conversation round and round and all inside a creepy silence as though the world's going to come to an end next second – he flinched, an infinitesimal fraction of a second before it came, as though there was an unendurable tension in the air which was about to snap.

It did, with a tearing crash that seemed to rip the room in half. Before he could glance at the roof to see if it was still on, there came another, and another; huge reports right over their heads with clear jagged edges that rounded and deepened as they bounced off the hills. They were followed, after a brief pause, by a pelting on the roof of what sounded like tile-cracking hail. Raindrops the size of golf-balls hit the small window. Edward ran to the passage, threw open the shutters and they looked down the valley that had been green and yellow when they walked along it this morning. Now it was obscured by a waist-level spray of the rain as it bounced from the ground. Between the spray and the black sky everything was preternaturally clear and across the clarity came lightning, very close, jagged flash after flash of it and then came another brief pause as though the sky was holding its breath and there bloomed between them and the village a brilliant circle, a ball of white fire that hung in front of them and then a crash that seemed to split the world. William felt the top of his head wet and touched it with his fingers, he wouldn't have been surprised to see blood. He stepped back and a drop of water the size of an eggcup hit the floortiles, followed by another. Edward swore and dashed for a bucket. 'Here!' William cried, and 'Here!' as more leaks sprang in the roof. They ran from room to room moving furniture, books; in the middle of William's bed there was already a puddle; he grabbed his notebook and wondered where to put it, he decided under the stove and rushed there as though it was his last resource in the drowning world. Buckets, saucepans, towels, already sodden blankets, anything that came to hand they put under the leaks that had started in every room; they were wet through themselves, and drops fell into the buckets so hard they splashed over the edge. Then, as quickly as it had come, it stopped. The dripping into the buckets slowed from machine-guns to the ticking of grandfather clocks, then slower, then silence. Outside was silence. Now there was another kind of mist as the ground steamed; the air, filtered through water, had become so pure that houses a mile away, shining, steaming, they felt they could almost touch.

William had not enjoyed himself so much since he had come to Italy and Edward was moving briskly, emptying buckets, replacing them under the still occasional drip, wringing out towels. 'Wow!' he said. And William said 'I shan't need a bath now.' He pushed open the front door and brightness streamed in; though most of the sky was still dark there was a huge mist of brightness where the sun somewhere was. The stony track that wound up to the road was pitted with bubbling yellow rivers, and at the foot of the steps that led up to the front door a small lake shone.

'An apple core, a view – a thunderstorm ...' said William.

Edward said 'Shall we go?'

'Can we get out?'

Mud to the knees they reached the road, the back wheels spurting the track all over them as they took it in turns to push the car from behind.

The town was deserted, as though the rain had washed the people away. The small shops were open, empty of customers. It began to rain again, but more gently. They pushed through the beaded strings that hung across the door of a little grocer's which had dark, delicious-looking hams hanging from the ceiling, and Edward delivered a shopping-list. Then they went to the bar on the empty main square, puddles on the green-painted iron table outside, and there were the people, the men anyway, so crowded together they steamed. Pretty outside, inside it was high and gaunt and the men stood on the dirty concrete floor and shouted at each other, their voices echoing. It was cold and cheerless and lit by flickering tubes of icy neon.

The men seemed excited by the wetness, stood in long plastic macintoshes staring out through the misted glass doors, turning to each other to shout and gesture, walking about frowning and returning to emphasise a point. It was as though they were not quite at ease to be within-doors in a place that was not their home, and felt the need to perform. All the men performed. Card-players at the side of the vast gymnasium-like structure drew cards from their hands as thought extracting a dagger from a sheath, raised them slowly above their shoulders and then, from somewhere behind their ears, brought them down on the table with a huge swing and a smack. At the end of the game the new dealer messed up the cards on the table immediately the last card had been played, in a small silence; then all the players began to shout at each other. An extraordinary number of them were mis-shapen, or unusually ugly, and the girl behind the cash-desk had shadows under her eyes dark as bruises; perhaps they were bruises.

Edward and William sat against a wall at the back drinking marsala. They also steamed. Edward listened, his neck elongated, straining to catch pieces of dialect, smiling when he did so. William understood nothing shouted by the hoarse echoing voices. He felt as though he had been drinking for a week. He was cold and getting colder. He had wanted to get back to the outside world and here, phantasmagorically, it was. Edward and he were washed up as on a reef. The storm, and the getting wet, the struggle with the car, their foreignness here in this café, brought them together. Edward gave up trying to understand the Tuscan and retracted his neck. They were in a place too dismal, too far from home, not to be grateful for each other's company. Even their drink was disgusting, though Edward seemed to like it and William felt no need to change it, or change anything, to sit anywhere else or leave or stay. That is what had been wrong; he had been trying to change Edward. Ludicrous. All argument is ludicrous. The strutting arguers in the bar – turning, stalking away, returning to deliver the *coup de grâce*, then leaning back, hands pressed against shoulders, palms turned outwards, to admire the effect of their thrust – it was all theatre, bad theatre. He had been guilty of theatricals with Edward, attempting to justify the ways of God to man. He knew nothing of the ways of God. He looked round the room with dismay, feeling the chill rise up his trousers from the damp concrete floor, and found it impossible to believe God had the smallest interest in this posturing male mass. They were too cocky. He preferred the huddled drinkers of Ireland, the slump of their silent backs acknowledged the victory of the rain. How dreary it was, this compulsive exhibition of maleness, and not even in the presence of women!

Perhaps they were ashamed of their sham little town.

Five hundred years ago the wealthy had begun to vie with each other to find who could build the tallest house. The result was a fantasy of thin towers which from a distance looked exquisite but, close-to in the rain, looked absurd and cruel. Italy was a sham! It depended on sun. In the open the assertiveness of these men would have been diluted by space, the towers like windowed needles would look graceful in the sun. Now they were black and silly and the grace of the men, enclosed, was seen for what it was, a mother's-boy cockiness. At least the Irish drinkers knew the sun could not be relied on …

Staring down into his glass, swirling the stickiness round the sides and watching it slowly drifting to the bottom, William acknowledged that his inveterate hopefulness was based on despair, whereas Edward's despair was derived from disappointed hopefulness. Of the two ways he preferred Edward's, but he put his money on his own.

'They seem all surface, these people' he said.

'It's not so bad when you understand what they're saying.'
'What are they saying?'
'Oh – football.'
'Really! I must have a cognac. You?' He got up, shaking his damp trousers from his calves, and ordered the same *marsala al uovo* and an Italian brandy for himself, determined to exchange a few words with these men. There was a coloured photograph of the local football team pinned by the wall-telephone and he recognised the name of one of the players; he had been born in Cardiff. 'Chinaglia? Si!' said a man next to him at the bar, and became voluble. By signs and the few words he knew, William learned, or hoped he learned, the position of their team in the league, their prospects, and one or two things he didn't quite follow. He became the centre of a group, they were very friendly and noisy and he left the bar, after many farewells, on a wave of goodwill. He returned, carrying the drinks, flushed. 'They're not such bad fellows.'

Edward had been watching the performance and said, seriously: 'Wherever I've been, and whatever I've done, I've always felt completely absurd.'

This was sufficiently near William's own experience for him to want to take it away like a bone to mumble over, but he put down the drinks and sat. There had been moments when he hadn't felt absurd: Beryl; his love for Peter when he was a child; his accident; in the field with Beryl ... 'So have I, usually. I haven't helped you much, have I.'

'Once when I was in England I went to see the Leonardo cartoon. I was in a bad way, pretty low. On the steps of the National Gallery I said a prayer. I said, "Leonardo, out of your great wisdom, help me!" and a very high, very reedy voice replied, "Do it yourself!"'

William banged the table, delighted, and Edward went on. 'I didn't expect you to help me. Anyway, perhaps you have. When one's younger one thinks people have wisdom – but it can't be passed on like gardening hints. There's example I suppose, and yours hasn't been too good. I've been watching you look at these people, hating them!'

'Ah, that's because I can't understand what they say, you see.'

'Whereas the willows talk your language.'

'They sound familiar.'

The sun came out in the square outside, wet stones shone. There was a putting on of coats and macintosh caps, except among the card-players who went on shouting and slapping their cards, oblivious. They went out into the now golden square, blinking. The towers around were black fingers against an insupportably bright sky.

The grocer's was full of women in black dresses; they too had emerged, now the rain was gone. Edward and William collected two carrier-bags the grocer had filled for them and William paid, wincing at the amount; it had cost him more than he could afford to come to Italy. 'Promise me you'll eat all this before you bump yourself off,' he said, and Edward did not smile. 'That was a joke' he said apologetically. Really, William thought, I don't think suicide should be taken all *that* seriously.

The new gas cylinder was already in the boot of the car, to William's puzzlement, who had forgotten about it. The grocer had carried it up the hill and put it there, a gentle courtesy that made William warm to that country.

It was evening, and suddenly cold, they had seen the last flare of the sun before it settled behind the hills, and they set off for Chiavelli. William had not understood how long their drive was to be, nor had he imagined how beautiful.

They climbed, catching the sun again, the sky a thickened evening blue while on the hilltops above them ruined towers were grey and gold. The fields were rounds and scoops among trees, so neat they looked as though they had been cut by scissors.

It was dark when they arrived at the house, a clear, cloudless dark filled with flower scents after the rain and the night noises of cicadas, nightingales, frogs. The house, half-way down a sloping grove of olives, showed up oddly bare, its silhouette stark and unsoftened.

There were expensive cars in the gravelled sweep; the new door with enormous ornamental nails in it was half-open and Edward beat on it with his fists, knuckles would clearly have been useless. A girl came out, half-exclaiming, half-giggling and embraced Edward, treating William as if he were an old friend too. 'You *are* dirty. Wasn't it exciting this afternoon.'

She was wearing a transparent white blouse and a long blue skirt. The blouse she drew attention to at once, opening her arms and laughing: 'Aren't I awful! We've been dressing up.' William thought he had never seen anybody so beautiful.

Inside various people were sitting round a table lackadaisically eating and drinking. It was all very haphazard and expensive. William was introduced and several pairs of eyes flicked over him and continued their conversation.

He sat on a bed and talked to a red-faced man who, like the rest of the company, was English: he managed a farm for a local grandee. 'Il principe!' he kept shouting. He approved of William's muddy trousers but seemed angry to be there at all and occasionally threw back his head and roared the verse of a dirty Rugby song. No one took any notice.

Emma, the beautiful girl who had welcomed them – it seemed this was her party – was dancing with a tall young actor who was as beautiful as she was. He leaned his forehead on hers as they danced and stared down at her exposed breasts in a kind of vertigo. This seemed to incense the farm manager who began snorting and confiding in William. 'Her Dad's in a bin. The Captain. Daddy's the only one she loves. Her heart belongs to Daddy – Da da da da da da da daddy a. I bet the old Principe gets his mitts on her. Old Nick. Not really. Yes he is. Nippy sod!' The manager fell back on the enormous cushions and went to sleep. A blond man in a grey linen suit began to wander round with a black overripe banana sticking out of his trousers. William addressed himself to another man, equally elegant. He mentioned a mutual acquaintance. 'I hate him,' said the man and moved away. People began to change clothes. Emma, to William's regret, appeared in a dinner jacket and a bow tie. The man who hated their mutual acquaintance was now in a flowered frock, make-up and high-heeled shoes and was being besought by the wife of the banana man to come back home with them. Her husband stood by smiling, his mouth open, his eyes never leaving the other man's face. 'Do! Do!' his wife kept saying excitedly.

The farm manager grunted in his sleep, nearly suffocated by the cushion, and William wandered outside.

Immediately he was not so much enveloped as hit by the space and stillness of the open hillside. He stood at the edge of a low newly-built wall watching the fireflies, feeling like a huge black star in the milky way. He listened to the frogs and the regular insect noises and felt contented, accompanied. One day he would discover why this always was. He looked down the slope over the tops of olive trees; there was not another house for miles – a scene unchanged for five hundred years, until now. *Lo scrisse Dante* ... He stood on concrete, he now sat on the new wall. There was a shape at his shoulder he could not decipher. He went to see what it was, it loomed up: a bull-dozer. He was on the floor of an enormous swimming-pool in process of being gouged from the old farm's olive grove. There were already changing rooms, a long pool-side cocktail bar in marble, the joints still roughly plastered. He saw in a huge mound the roots of olive trees that had been grubbed out.

Tired, he closed his eyes and nearly fell, became aware of the danger of being sick. He went to their car and squeezing himself into a corner of the back seat was soon asleep. He was partly woken by a rhythm of car doors slamming, engines revving, and became fully awake when a warm, scented presence climbed in beside him. Emma. She laced her arm into his and he felt her warmth along his side.

How pleasant it was! He was mildly surprised by Edward, the back of whose neck looked determined as they drove through the dawn. Presumably he was abducting her and she had sat in the back to make it look less obvious. She snuggled into William's shoulder, half-dozing, half-chatting to them both, a girl who liked giving pleasure.

Perhaps she would thaw out Edward. The look of the back of his neck made that seem unlikely. The replies he gave, eyes on the twisting road, were short and matter-of-fact, as though to a sister, or an accomplice.

William found her delightful; indiscriminate as a puppy. He was young again, in the back of a car with a new girl; he had forgotten how nice it was.

The journey ended too soon, in pink dawn at the farm. She wanted the party to continue, insisted they have some brandy together before they went to bed. They sat round the table drinking; she illuminated the kitchen, chattering, giggling. Edward said little, filling their glasses. William tried to leave them together but they both besought him not to, as though they were afraid of being left alone. Then Edward without warning rose, said he was going to bed, and left.

Emma seemed barely to notice; turned her full attention to William. William guessed that she and Edward had reached no arrangement at the party. Finding she was alone in that house, owned by her absent boyfriend, he had offered to put her up. She existed for her effect on others and was now afraid to go to her room and be alone. William stood, 'Well ...' he said, still undecided. She looked up, her smile gone. Here was another presence abandoning her. He saw he was only a presence, undifferentiated — how would he have been otherwise, old fool! — and he allowed cowardice to triumph. 'I must be off,' he said. 'Have you everything you want?' 'Yes of course' she said, looking down, with the faintest parody of his householder tone. 'Goodnight.' She took a lamp from the table and turned, humming, towards the room Edward had told her earlier, with some emphasis, was hers. She left the door open, still humming as she moved about inside it while William stood thinking about her, holding his lamp in the dark kitchen although the day was already lightening outside. 'Goodnight,' he said, turning to go to his own room and did not hear a reply, although the humming stopped suddenly.

At lunch time she was about again, singing, washing-up, Simon and Garfunkel on the gramophone, wearing an old white shirt of Edward's knotted round her middle, even her bare feet handsome and practical. She could eat us all for breakfast thought William, and noticed Edward treated her differently, like a favourite sister now, cadaverously grinning. He hoped they had made some contact during what had been left of the night, it was a waste of such a creature not to be used, when she so much wanted to be.

He went unsteadily with a red-eyed Edward to gather some logs in the wood.

'Is Emma going to stay here for some time?'

'Until her boyfriend gets back, I suppose.'

'What's he like?'

'Gervase? He's all right. An Irish milord. She's not his only girlfriend. I think they're on the point of breaking up anyway.'

'What'll she do?'

'Live on her wits.'

'Will you take her on?'

'God no! I'm not rich enough. You have to be *very* rich for Emma. Can you manage this one? I'll put it on end. If you can get your shoulder under the top and I'll lever it up.'

The fallen tree was heavy, it hurt William's shoulder, and they staggered with it back to the house, William leading, Edward talking to his back. 'It's awful. Worse than with Helen. She only exists to give pleasure.'

'What's so awful about that?'

'She can't receive any. The only person she's close to is her father and he's sick so that makes him sort of sacred. She just watches you the whole time to see if she's working on you. You have to keep reassuring her. She's a dish of poisoned sweets. Though I reckon some of her boyfriends only like poisoned sweets.'

'And you?'

'It's such a bloody waste. She's so fantastically beautiful. All that equipment for pleasure and she can't really give it because she can't receive it. What's the use of the beauty then?'

'Do you mind if we put this thing down?'

They did so in sight of the house and sat on it, William rubbing his shoulder, feeling shaky. 'I honestly believe you expect me to answer that question.'

'Why not. You're always going on about beauty and messages and inklings and all that. Here's somebody who's just about perfect to look at – have you ever seen anybody better-looking, sexier?'

'No.'

' ... and an hour with her is like being in the wine-press. The screw goes down tighter and tighter. "Amuse me, am I amusing, what can we do that's more amusing? Who can I find who will be more amused by me?"'

'She's not the only person who's hung-up on her dad.'

'How do you mean?'

'You. *I'm* not your dad. Christ, *I* don't know! Anything you like. Original Sin. Don't bash me over the head with your difficulties. It's simple: if you want to survive don't get involved with coffin-nails like Emma – if that's what she is. If you don't want to survive don't grab Emma and say, "Look, there's no point in this girl I've grabbed and everything's pointless I told you so." Don't try to have it both ways.'

'You do.'

'Yes by God I do. But the both ways I have it make me want to live more whereas the both ways you have it make you not want to live at all! Which gets the wooden spoon?'

Edward sat on the log making a noise as though laughing.

'As a matter of fact,' said William, 'I think you're well-suited.'

'I'm hollow too?'

'Perhaps she isn't either. You could be a good double-act, two desperados together.'

'I'm not rich enough.'

'No you aren't. You weren't rich enough for Helen either. Emma wants money. So do you. She's better looking. It's a hard world.'

'What do you do for cash William – I've often wondered?'

'Try to like things that aren't expensive.'

'So you don't need to bother.'

'Of course I bother! People who trust to luck get kicked. You've trusted to luck, you've ended up thinking there's no point in trying – if you have ended, which I doubt.'

'That's not quite true – about not trying.'

'Just think what Emma would be like if she believed in

God,' said William, 'She'd make the most marvellous whore.'

Surprise made Edward laugh. 'She might be a nun,' he said.

William considered the possibility and didn't reject it. 'Anyway, she wouldn't drive herself potty looking for reassurance.'

'So God exists to warm up tarts?'

'Certainly.'

'How very comfortable.'

It was a heavy day, overcast. There was a generalised brightness that hurt the eyes more than direct sun. They sat on the log side by side, large brown ants crawling over their boots. William looked down at them, hearing his shallow breathing caused by the log-carrying, exasperation and too much to drink all week.

Edward turned to him grinning, unoffended, and William looked at him bleakly. ' "Our saints are poets, Milton, Blake, who would rib men with pride against the spite of God",' he suddenly quoted. ' "Celt, your saints adorn the poor with roses and praise God for standing still." Unpopular idea that. I'm a Celt. Pity I have to get back today.' They picked up the log. 'We've given each other a hard time.'

'I'll miss you.'

'Let's get drunk at lunch. I'm in love with your Emma. Don't forget the policeman.'

'My God!'

'Why not take Emma along, she'd bowl him over?'

'Mistake. The more he fancied her the more he'd punish us. He believes in God you see.'

'Poor Emma. And all she wants is to be useful.'

William sat on the green plastic seat of his couchette and regretted his asperity with Edward. But it was probably because Emma, by whose presence he still felt himself pleasantly affected – she had kissed him on parting – represented what he could only call his view of life: which was that all appearances are deceptive but should not be blamed; we should blame our own eagerness to be deceived.

Anyway, they aren't all that deceptive. Emma's undoubted beauty had to be fuelled, however uncertainly, from within. It wasn't just a bloom. And she reminded him that under the hard surfaces of the world, indeed under our own minds, there lay the patient beauty which was responsible for our odd spurts of faith and disinterestedness, otherwise they were inexplicable; and responsible for our aberrations also, because these insights received, and then removed, made us savage and cruel. So at least William believed and he was grateful for the potence of Emma's effect on him.

A large bespectacled Englishman filled the carriage with the delicious smells of his picnic. An elderly Italian peasant woman in black sat in a corner trying not to cry.

The Englishman, his mouth and chins decorated by breadcrumbs, offered her food and wine desperately, as though to cork her up. She refused and sat staring out of the window. A young Italian girl moved next to her and asked her what was the matter.

At last the old lady got out and the Englishman, who had been making humming noises, jerking his head round the carriage as though looking for escape, said 'Oof! Do tell us what was the matter with Mother Hubbard?' The Italian girl told him her blind son had just been committed to an institution. 'All very sad,' he said, 'but why does she have to tell *us*!' The girl turned away, disgusted.

Eric, as he asked his travelling companions to call him, was not to be put off. Soon he involved everyone in the determination of his enjoyment. In the evening he performed an elaborate toilet, changing into striped Winceyette pyjamas, and at what William nervously hoped was a long halt he allowed Eric to entice him onto the platform for a drink at the bar. He was a striking sight on the station, red-faced, portly, his pyjamas now covered by a very tired silk dressing-gown with dragons on it. A policeman gravely regarded them. 'Poof! I've had more policemen than hot dinners!' He shot the policeman a winning smile. To William's astonishment the policeman smiled flirtatiously back.

He drank brandies and talked of himself: he lived in the *unfashionable* part of Norwood. The platform emptied, William heaved him up the carriage steps among slamming doors and waving flags. 'Never missed a train in my life' he puffed as William pushed him along the corridor.

He made a tremendous performance of climbing into his bunk, finding the small ladder unnegotiable, subsiding, swearing, giggling. William noticed the blankets on the disapproving Italian girl's bed were shaking, she was laughing helplessly.

In the morning he sat on the station drinking coffee, waiting for his connection. Eric had stumbled off protesting eternal friendship, gesturing. He had spent a week in the company of a man who apparently refused to enjoy anything, presumably because of the existence of blind boys and bereft mothers; and eighteen hours in the company of a man who was determined to enjoy everything, and Eric had cheered him up, sent a girl to sleep laughing. Pleasure is difficult, its achievement a creative act. Edward wanted to spit in God's eye. It was too far to spit.

A waiter was tidying up the ashtrays on the other tables, emptying them into a bigger one. He banged the ashtrays back on the metal tables in William's ear, tried to remove his unfinished cup. He was called from inside the bar and dumped the overflowing ashtray on William's table as he passed, leaving him looking into it. William picked up the piece of paper on his table, counted out the exact money, picked up the ashtray, went to the bar and plonked it down. He paid the waiter. 'Service n'est pas compris, monsieur.' 'Quel service?' said William heavily, and stumped out.

Pleasure is a creative act, therefore an aggressive one; it imposes itself on experience. He should have said that to Edward.

There was a post office on the station and William sent a cable to Peter in America, paying for it with his last francs. PLEASE COME ALL FOUR WANT TO SEE YOU LOVE WILLIAM.

8

Edward stood high in the crook of the tall cherry tree and reached out dangerously. 'Are you there? Get ready to catch.'

'Wait a minute.' He heard a scrambling beneath him as Emma got up from where she had been lying and pushed through the long grass to the other side of the tree. 'All right. I'm underneath you with my hat out. Fire away.'

'For heaven's sake don't miss them, when they're bruised they don't keep. And *stay* there, don't go away again.'

'Edward darling, we've been at this for hours.'

'Just stay there.' He balanced carefully to cut the bunch of shining cherries, cream-coloured on one side, dark red where the sun had reached them, with his long-handled secateurs. It was awkward work, with a spice of danger. All the trees were old, too long unpruned, and the cherries grew far out. 'Here they come.'

'Oops!' She caught them deftly in her pink straw hat. She was like a cherry herself, he thought, looking down; her skin was the same texture. 'Is that the lot?' She called up.

'Good God no! Look and see.'

'Oh really Edward, I've had enough. Let's go to Siena for lunch – you promised.'

'Did I?'

'You know you did. The cherries can wait. I'm going in to change. I'll take the basket.'

The cherries could not wait, the birds had opened too many and wasps were burrowing into them. He had already been stung twice and his bare arm was beginning to swell where a caterpillar had poisoned him, or an ant. It was a valuable crop and needed to be saved but he couldn't do it with only Emma to help him who didn't like doing anything, except cooking and housework. She did those things with a sort of child-bride briskness that depressed him: she was making the place nice for Daddy. Everything else was Daddy's job.

The farm had never been in a worse state and what little money he had left was being spent on long lunches in Florence and Siena. He now even had to buy petrol on tick that he had no idea how he was going to pay. He was interested to see when the crash would come, and what form it would take. A wasp almost disappeared inside a wrecked cherry, becoming still and self-absorbed as it fed, then moved to the next one, leaving the wreck. Emma would float innocently elsewhere because naughty Edward wouldn't buy her a bow-wow. Wouldn't, couldn't, it made no difference to Emma. She bored and irritated him and her happy greed seemed to him sensible. It was justice that the last of his sweetness, or rather, the farm's, which was really Helen's leftover, should go to satisfy the helpless craving of a creature like Emma. She could do him no damage he had not already done himself.

Helen had worked hard, sweating, turning herself into a farmer's wife so determinedly that he had sickened. In front of his eyes she had grown a beard and biceps and a deep gruff voice. In fact the masculinity had only come into her face – and the dependent femininity gone out of it – when she looked at him; when without complaint she shouldered another burden that should have been his. She could cope better, or at least quicker, so he became useless. In order, as she thought, to save the farm, she had destroyed him. But there are more ways of coping than hers. Her whole life had become bills, plans. He had wanted the farm and their marriage to grow round them, like cherries fattening. That was not such a bad idea. It was what he had in common with William. But William was an adept at having the best of both worlds, from everything, politics, religion, relationships, he only took what suited him. For all his talk of Grace and God and so on he knew instinctively which side his bread was buttered. Whereas he, Edward was a disaster. And a bad-tempered bastard. He had watched his appalling savagery to Helen with astonishment, almost with disbelief.

But a man has a right to be a disaster. It's a kind of career not much different from any other except in terms of personal comfort. Helen's obsession with balancing the budget was absurd and she had had to give up: his insistence on life as a slow process of growth was also absurd because it had created its own travesty, a sort of elephants' graveyard round the house. He looked down at it now from his tree, barely seeing it because he was so used to it, but each of those abandoned chassis had been a good idea at the time. Besides, they had a beauty. Were no worse, certainly, than rows of bedding-plants laid out in rows each year, nature regimented into decoration. These cars had had to do with men, had use and therefore dignity.

There were the bones outside the house too, bought to feed the dogs and the pigs. He'd killed the pigs and eaten them. The dogs had been poisoned or shot by the weekend hunters who came from Florence to slaughter the birds. Their bones lay elsewhere presumably. All except the black bitch.

Up on the road at the top the windows of a charabanc flashed as it swung down the hill past the huge roadside advertisement with CYNARA written on it in red and blue. Some men had planted it on his – Helen's – property one day, trampling juniper bushes. He had always meant to remove it. Since then others had appeared all down the road; as the traffic multiplied so did they. To the south of his tree he could see the little battlemented hill town three miles away which he could not have seen last year because the olive trees had been in the way. Now, the olives felled, the terraces levelled, his concrete vine-posts gave the impression of marching to the horizon, marching in line with the diminishing posts of other larger vineyards right up the hill on top of which the little town sat. Permanent sprays of water arched above them, catching the sun as they turned over the grey lines of posts that made the whole place for miles look like a war cemetery. He would never put in the vines to match his posts. The government subsidy had been spent. William had been right to be sceptical when he had mentioned his plans, boasting. He had opened the farm to the south and exposed it to no purpose. He could see the grey asbestos roof of the furniture factory now, and turning to the west he could see on another hill the deserted village of Alba, roofless, almost invisible against the rocks of the hill as though a light had gone out of the stones of the empty houses; all the people there had descended the hill to work in the furniture factory, or had deserted their own vineyards to find work as labourers in the big ones.

William watched the world wryly, and said his prayers. Edward had fought. Those concrete posts had been a good idea. He had not enjoyed the felling of the olives, or the loss of the huge spanish chestnut – the bulldozer had been through the roots before he could save it – but he had fought, and lost.

But he would gather in the cherry harvest. What he really needed was Orissi and his trailer; underneath the trees, ladder on the trailer, they could reach the outer branches which were bending under the fruit. But Orissi would have to be paid his share of the crop and anyway he was busy with his own trees which were not so good. Perhaps he could stretch a tarpaulin below the branches and drop the cherries without too much damage? He noticed a bunch near at hand and began to eat them, spitting the stones through the branches at the approaching figure of Emma, crisply dressed in white material, little pleats in front making her look demure. Yet she'd come all those weeks ago with so little luggage. And her hair was as shiny and curly as ever, even in the morning when they woke up; she seemed to have to take no care of herself at all.

'Aren't you going to change?'
'I'm not coming.'
'Of course you are.'
'I've no money.'
'That's all right, we'll manage.'
'How?'
'I can't talk to you up there. Do come down.'

A picture of himself up a tree saying 'Shan't' weakened Edward. He swung on a branch and landed at her feet. A mistake: he could not climb back into the tree now.

'If we go to Alfredo's we'll probably bump into Il Principe.'

'If we don't?'

'We'll manage, stop fussing. You can't go like that.'

'I can.'

'Oh well, let's hurry then. What's the matter with your arm?'

'A caterpillar peed on it.'

At a more convenient time she would have rushed for ointment, made much of him, Daddy's girl. Now she wanted lunch. 'I've brought the car key. You'd better roll down your sleeve, it looks ghastly.'

As they drove off Emma said: 'Is it true you have no money?'

On the way to Siena Edward stopped at the local post office to pick up the letters. There was only one, from Helen's lawyers. They always said depressing and aggressive things. He put it in his pocket.

Alfredo's was very good and very expensive. Near the Campo in Siena it was the roofed-in courtyard of an ancient palazzo, walls set with busts and medallions and in the centre among flowing greenery was the cool sound of water; from a lion's head with a lead pipe in its mouth water still fell into the old courtyard well. There was a pleasant impression, while enclosed, of being in the open air. The tables were widely spaced on the worn tile floor and Emma after she had ordered, and devoured a few gri-sticks, seemed ready for a brisk chat about business. She treated him, he noticed, for the first time like an equal. 'Is it true you have no money, really none?'

'Really none.'

'What are you going to do?'

'Sell the cherry crop.'

'Will that bring in much?'

'No.'

'You can raise money on the farm.'

'It's Helen's.'

'You can't live on *nothing*.'

'You do.'

'I'm a girl.'

'Yes. Is Gervase coming back?'
'I haven't heard.'
'What are *you* going to do?'

She shrugged and laughed. 'Can't you get somebody to help on the farm?'

'Instead of you?'

'I haven't been much use.'

'You cook well.'

'You *are* sweet. Only because I'm greedy. This is super, try some.' She pronged a couple of ravioli and pushed them towards his mouth. He pulled his head away, fascinated by the new business-like Emma; he couldn't take tit-bits from a fellow-conspirator. She clearly had a plan, she was possibly going to offer him the role of pimp.

After a plate of *carbonara* Edward did not feel hungry and drank wine, thinking of cherries. He was past wondering who would pay for the meal. Emma ate enormously, a Florentine steak as big as her plate, a sorbet, cream cake, cheese. She ate every meal as though it might be her last.

He found her looking past his head with a joyous expression 'Ugo!' she cried, and there was Il Principe himself, his grey jacket round his shoulders, his nose sharp, his black hair brushed back from his bony forehead. He sat at their table, after a smiled enquiry to both of them, ordering some wine in a soft mutter the waiter seemed to understand intuitively, rushing off almost before he had finished. He crumbled bread and smiled, looking at both of them with his soft eyes. 'You are shopping?' He spoke in English.

'Eating,' said Emma.

'You must eat some more.'

Emma giggled. 'I've eaten Edward into bankruptcy already!'

Lazily, very friendly, he brought his eyes to Edward's, no enquiry in them. 'It does us good to see you. Eh? A sorbet? A gateau? Come, you are my guests, both of you.' The waiter arrived, breathless, with the wine.

Ugo spoke quietly to him, making a small circular gesture with his finger, including Edward. 'You permit me?' It was done.

People and Weather

The wine was a good bottle from his own vineyard. He filled their glasses, filling his own with mineral water from their bottle. Although he appeared to do this at normal speed he gave the sense of doing it in slow-motion. He sat back and took out his cigarette case in the same way, then his lighter, then he opened the case. Edward guessed that if he had been a woman he might have been excited by the way Ugo appeared to be willing to take infinite trouble, infinite time. All his hand movements were slightly curved, caressing. 'You don't mind?' he said, taking out a cigarette and tapping it lightly on the case. 'Only tobacco I'm afraid.' He smiled at Emma, indulgent. Just so would Emma's dream of a Daddy behave.

It was the way he had behaved when they visited him, and he had also suggested cruelty too. Perhaps Emma would like that? 'Il Principe's a darling' she had said: 'You must come.' His house was done out like a London club, except the leather-covered chairs were hard as though no one had ever sat on them and the sets of leather-covered books looked new. There was a sense of a genuine rootedness that was unlived. Edward guessed Ugo and his family normally lived in Rome.

There were two other girls there, both were pretty and both appeared to be recovering from, or about to have, nervous breakdowns. One of them Ugo teased throughout dinner with consistent sadism till she sat staring at her plate with red spots on her cheeks.

Afterwards they sat on the hard leather chairs and drank drinks from a trolley, mixed with great care by Ugo. They smoked marihuana, passed round from his case deprecatingly, as though he apologised for being so obvious. He disappeared for a while to his bedroom, which led off from where they were sitting, to take his drops, he explained, first asking for the key to his medicine-chest from the fair, teased girl. It was clearly a ritual. He stood over her unmoving while she fumbled desperately in her enormous bag, her hair falling forward and covering it like a tent. He took it from her without a word and strode rapidly to his room leaving the door open. At least one place in the house was not hard and shiny; Edward saw black hangings softly illuminated by concealed lights.

When he came back conversation had languished and he suggested a film. Emma had told Edward about the films. 'What would you like' he said gently to the girls. 'Leses, foursomes, leather, doggies?'

'Oh you are rotten, Ugo. You know I love doggies,' said Emma.

'Doggies then,' said Ugo, shrugging. He pressed a bell and the man who had served them at dinner appeared. Ugo said they were not to be disturbed and the man nodded and left, after drawing the curtains.

Ugo inserted a cassette into a console, pressed a button, and a large television set lit up among the books at the other end of the room.

The thin girls watched languidly, the fair one pulling at her mouth. Emma giggled sometimes and shifted, tossing, the inappropriate phrase occurred to Edward, her curls. As she watched the lights in her hair ought slowly to have dimmed.

'Better than the local station anyway,' Ugo murmured behind him.

'I daresay,' said Edward who had been thinking, unhappily, about boredom.

Ugo was bored now, in the restaurant, or pretending to be, and Edward wondered what his next move would be. He understood that a transfer was about to take place, now he had no money and Emma had nowhere else to go. He knew any breach of decorum, any hurry, on his part would lower Emma's value in Ugo's eyes, there had to be the appearance of conquest, and he did not want to spoil things for her.

Clearly Ugo was in no hurry. The property was so valuable he could afford to wait. Edward wanted the whole business over as soon as possible.

'What were you thinking of doing this afternoon?' said Ugo.

'I was thinking of going back to pick my cherries,' said Edward.

'The crop is good this year.'

'Too good. I'm afraid the price'll go down.'

'Ah ...' Ugo spread his hands and made a shrugging gesture with his chin — two farmers together, 'I was thinking ...'

'Yes?' said Emma.

He turned to her, gently reproachful, she had spoken too quickly. 'I have to visit my mother. Not very gay perhaps, but it would give her such pleasure to see your young face. And — he turned to Edward — 'there are one or two pictures you might enjoy.'

Edward thought quickly. If I say 'No' he won't take Emma to see his mother alone. Time will pass, it may be days before another take-over opportunity suggests itself and that means more endless lunches at bloody Alfredo's. 'The cherries can wait,' he said.

'You are sure? She is very old. Not much pleasure for you, but' — he cocked his head and shrugged again — 'we shall see.'

'I'll just settle the bill here,' said Edward, for form's sake.

'No no no no no.' Ugo shook his hand in front of his own face several times. 'It is all done.'

'But really ...'

'Ssh,' he smiled, turning to Emma. 'You have everything? My mother will love that dress. Carissima.' Emma walked in front of them. Both men watched her. Then Edward turned to Ugo who met his eyes, his face blank and innocent. 'After you,' he said, and they went out into the street.

As they walked Ugo was careful to treat them as a couple, he the third. He kept to Edward's side, addressing most of his remarks and directions to him. There was a confusing series of lefts and rights, Ugo's hand gently on his elbow. The narrow streets were airless, the smart little shops and the traffic asleep for the afternoon. At last they were in a leafy courtyard, with a fountain, and a polished bell-pull on the wall among the ivy. An old bent maid in black opened the door. 'Signorino!' 'Maria!' He introduced them.

Upstairs they were shown into a long narrow salon with high-backed chairs set about. Where the fireplace would have been in England there was a photograph of a senatorial figure with a split beard. 'My father,' said Ugo. 'Madre!' The old woman entered slowly, with a stick, a black shawl over her white hair. He kissed her carefully on both cheeks and they sat around her eating small cakes brought by the old maid and drinking thin tea she poured from a silver pot which had two pieces of paper hanging from it, tags for the tea bags.

Ugo was formal as a little boy at his First Communion, sitting upright, his knees together. After a while he asked Edward if he would like to see the pictures. 'I'm sure Mr Campion would be bored with those old things of ours,' the old lady said. 'However, go, go and stretch your legs away from my tea table, and smoke your cigarettes. Will you keep me company?' she said to Emma. 'I want to ask you the secret of your wonderful hair.' She touched her own and slightly adjusted her shawl to reveal more of it.

Outside the room they were in a long gallery that extended round four sides of a courtyard. The pictures were enormous and dark. Gilded scrolls at the bottom usually bore a famous name, Salvator Rosa, Annibale Caracci. Possibly.

'It was good of you to come.'

'I like your mother,' said Edward, truthfully.

'We shall go soon. Your cherries.' Ugo smiled in the gloom of the gallery. Edward was frowning, trying to discern the subject of the vast canvas above him. It seemed to be entirely black. 'You don't like pictures?'

'They are very fine,' he said flatly. Ugo stood looking sideways at him as though expecting something. Then he turned away, almost brusquely, giving up.

Edward was sorry for him. If I can continue to be as boring as this, he thought, he might leave me alone. But I'm not only trying to be boring, I am boring. I can think of nothing to say in this awful place that seems to have been designed for the passage of coffins.

They went back and the two women were chatting easily; Emma's Italian was good. He and Ugo stood and waited till his mother chose to notice them. 'You must go?' 'Alas!' There were the same careful kisses, farewells, the mother at the head of the stairs, the old bent maid with her head on the level of Ugo's waist showing them out, smiling knowingly.

Outside Ugo asked, 'Where is your car?' On the way to it they passed a small bar. 'Coffee?' he suggested, peering into the dark interior. 'Nino!' 'Ugo!' A young man in pearl grey, with yellow curls, stood at the bar sipping from a small cup. 'Emma! Carissima mia!' There were greetings, kisses, handshakes. Emma was giggling. No one ever seems to have any work to do, thought Edward, bad-temperedly, they stand around in bars creatively greeting. Now both the men were buying *gettone* for the bar telephone, summoning the gang to come here, in their open cars. Another mate rolled in: kisses, shouts. Emma was back home.

Taking a deep breath, expanding his chest, Edward raised both arms and twiddled his fingers, shouting above the hubbub 'Ciao! Ciao!' He pushed through to Emma, kissing her on both cheeks as Ugo had kissed his mother. 'I must go. Cherries. Be good.' She flung her arms round him, pressing her cheek against his. 'Isn't this fun?'

'Yes,' he said. 'You're back where I found you. More or less.'

'I've known all these people for *years*!'

'I know. They're nice.'

She giggled. 'Eduardo thinks you're nice,' she said to the pearl-grey man who was absently tossing liar dice in a leather cup.

'Claro,' he said, without looking at Edward and turned his heavy-lidded eyes to the door through which nobody was coming.

'See you then, Emma.'

'See you Edward.'

As he turned, oddly sad, Ugo stopped him. 'Cherries?' he said, solicitiously.

'Same old fruit.'

'We'll be having supper at Alfredo's. You'll join us?'

'I'd love to. I may be too sticky.'

'You have a telephone?'

'Afraid not.'

Ugo shook his head, as though stumped. He had wanted to keep a good look to things, telephone later, could Emma stay overnight, everyone else was, it had got late. Without a telephone how could he? He was holding Edward's arm, he looked genuinely concerned, his face very close. Edward wanted to say something simple, like 'She's yours for ten million lire' but he was frightened of fouling things up for Emma. He wanted to say 'She's no good in bed' but who knew what she'd be like with Il Principe?

But he couldn't corrupt Emma because he'd never reach her. Poor old Mephistopheles, he'd only be a naughty amusing man whatever he tried. Even drugs wouldn't work because she so hated feeling unwell. Edward hoped he wasn't physically cruel. Emma'd survive. 'I may see you tonight then,' he said.

'But you must.'

Backing away, the last fatuity, Edward found himself blowing a kiss. For the first time Ugo looked startled.

The car felt empty without her. He was glad he had left her with Italians. Their foreignness and apparent gaiety created just the right sort of distance; she would feel comfortable. An English or American devil might have understood her better.

Spinning the wheel round a sharp corner he felt the letter from Helen's lawyers in his pocket. They were always so formally nasty: 'access to children', 'lack of funds or prospects'. Her own letters to him were matter-of-fact, even friendly.

He felt remorse, he had been a bastard, but Helen had not been faultless either. Her hopes had been too easy and when they failed she had thought she could replace them by will, by hard work. Why should it have been his job to protect her illusions?

The thought of May bothered him, their daughter with the odd eye; she was so plain and fresh. Other children liked her. When they left her out of games because she could not see well it was done without spite – except from the odd cradle-bastard. What good could he have done her? We need people but to stay with people because we need people is bad medicine. We have to stay with a name, not with a strained brow, or a wonky eye. Helen had become a suffering forehead, even her eyebrows had thickened, as

People and Weather

though to support it. He had been severely depressed by those eyebrows, they were like a graph of the failure of the farm, but he had not mentioned this because she would have plucked them, as she would have totted up an account, or fed the pigs, as a part of her duty.

The thought of May could make him swerve the car.

Arriving back he stayed sitting in it, looking at the farmhouse. Its yellow stones looked grey and heavy, the light was on the cherry trees behind him. He had been reasonable, and reasonably honest: as a result here he was, alone, at the end of his rope. The posts of the projected new vineyard frightened him. They were the future and he had nothing to give it. He had so much wanted not to be like his father!

His father had been a Communist in his youth and then had given up, given up life. Took coals off the fire in the already dismally cold room and at nine o'clock every night yawned and said 'Well, I'm for my bed!' Edward's mother despised him, took to religion. In the end Edward had disappointed them both. They wanted something from him and he could never discover what, he spoke neither of their languages; as a result he doubted whether he spoke anybody's. He still did. Helen had looked at him sometimes so incomprehendingly.

Unlike his father he could face up to facts. He faced them now and his end didn't seem different. Whether he gave up on life didn't matter, it had given up on him. He had no idea how to get through the next days, never mind years. He could live on cherries for a bit he supposed. But he would face it, just as he would face the letter from Helen's Scottish lawyers, which he dreaded.

He opened it, sitting at the wheel, so afraid of it that he didn't understand at first. She had given him the farm. 'Life-rent', one word, got through to him. It belonged to the children but it was his until he died. It was generous of Helen. Probably she had not known what else to do with it.

He tried to think what difference it made, looking at the farmhouse, lighting a cigarette. He got out of the car, went up and touched it. 'A farmer.' 'My farm.' He tried the words out. All right. Possible.

Perhaps he could now borrow money on it, and get the vines in? He would go and see the British Consul, he would know. Nice chap. Helped him with that damned policeman: 'Harassing a national of ours.' In fact the Consul was an Italian. He could maybe become more ordinary, make friends with the neighbours, save up. He would grow a bit cracked walking round the farm talking to himself. Maybe he could get some students from England next spring? He was *damned* if he'd end up like Father! Damned.

I'll go and see Orissi.

He crossed the slopes to his neighbour's farm; amused because he found himself taking long strides, a lord of broad acres.

The family was sitting round a table outside, wife and daughters stoning cherries, Orissi sharpening the blades of his hay-cutter, a straw-bottomed fiasco on the table, a loaf and a plate of olives. It looked better than Alfredo's.

'I've come to ask if I can take Giovanni. I'm getting the cherries in. I need someone to hold the tarpaulin.' Giovanni was keeping the blade steady for his father.

'What do you say Giovanni?' his father asked him. The boy shrugged and Orissi turned to Edward. 'Of course he'll come, the young one. Have you many trees to do?'

'Twelve.'

He gave a few more scrapes to the blade and spoke to his wife in Tuscan, and she answered him, still rhythmically stoning the cherries. 'We'll all come with you,' he said.

Yesterday Edward would have protested, apologised. Now he said. 'I can't give you any of the crop. I need it.'

Orissi looked at him, expressionless. Then he shrugged and called out, climbing into his tractor. Two of the boys fastened on a trailer; the whole family was in action, climbing aboard.

They picked until it was dark. Edward looked down at Giovanni's upturned face, standing on the trailer, waiting for the cherries to be handed down to him. He had a bad eye too; not as bad as May's. They love it, he thought, or they don't think about it. Cherries are there to be picked, work to be done. I'll work. Life's easy if there's work to do,

Fairly easy.

Half the trees were done, the cherries stowed. The family gathered in the quickly falling dark. They had all been working since daybreak. They seemed untired, though hushed by the darkness.

From the seat of his revving tractor Orissi shouted: 'We'll come tomorrow. They mustn't waste.'

'Yes.' Edward paused; he remembered his earlier feeling, of being a farmer. Settled on his feet he looked up at Orissi. 'You've helped me.'

Orissi turned back to him, Edward couldn't see his face. With one hand he switched on his headlights and the other he raised slowly in acknowledgement, Edward could see it outlined against the last green of the sky, then he let it fall slowly, with a slightly curved gesture, like Ugo's.

The mother sat upright in the trailer, eating cherries, spitting the stones over the side with a small movement of her head. The children huddled together, drawing pieces of sacking over themselves against the evening chill. Dew was falling. Slowly, bumping, the tractor drew away, the mother still sitting upright, bracing herself with her legs.

'Ciao Eduardo.'

'Ciao. Ciao.'

9

The grey cliffs of Dover welcomed William. A foreigner, he never came back without excitement. The customs men looked avuncular, the horrible tea on Victoria Station suited him. It was the prosaic nature of England that he admired, because poetry was rooted in it. In less settled countries you don't get poetry you get protest songs. Clever young Englishmen should not be too impatient with their native orderliness, they should know how fragile it is – they should value their poets.

Thus did South American Celtish William, honorary Englishman, look out of the train window at rows of little red houses in the rain and lecture his almost-compatriots. He had spent a disturbed night in the couchette, woken for ticket examination at every frontier and by Eric cumbrously climbing from his bunk, twice, to go to the lavatory; he had indigestion from a brandy on the boat.

His feeling for Emma had slowly become translated into an urgent longing to see Beryl. In all their years together he had never told her how much she meant to him. Even a short absence had reminded him. He would tell her the moment he got back.

When they died, were they tied together forever? What they felt for each other, wherein it was true and a growth towards God, would exist and still grow. But he would want her physical presence. If that was possible what about the octillions of other souls standing dazzled in the presence of God? *In my Father's house there are many mansions, if it were not so I would have told you.*

Was that a reassurance about the extent of the accommodation?

William had his hand over his eyes, temporarily dazzled by all those souls; he became enclosed in dark and took it away, gratefully looking down at the British Railways table, and looking forward to Victoria Station. At least he knew what he must do as soon as he arrived.

As a preliminary he had another brandy in the station buffet, hoping it would fight the first one and win. Then, his suitcase weighing heavy, he took a bus to Putney. It would look odd, arriving at Beryl's nursing home with a suitcase, as though urgently; he hoped the matron had prepared her.

It was not a bad place: two large Victorian houses with a garden at the back, and not too expensive although it was more than they could afford.

The muscular matron opened the door. 'We're upstairs in the TV Lounge and *so* looking forward to seeing you. We're not sure we're quite ready though, a day or two wudnae do us any harm.'

Beryl would have spent the last days in bed, sedated; tiredness was unlikely to be her problem.

'I'll just put your bag in my cubby-hole,' she said, taking an enormous bunch of keys from her pocket. 'Some of us have light fingers.' She made to lead up the stairs.

'I wonder if you'd ...?' said William, wishing to see Beryl alone.

The Matron paused at the bottom of the stairs, her smile gone. 'Mind you don't go tiring us now,' she called after him.

He stopped outside a brown-painted door with a white enamel plaque which said *TV Lounge*. He paused for a moment, then knocked; there was no reply. Turning the handle gently he opened the door and put his head inside. A blank television screen faced him and behind it, silhouetted against the window, was Beryl, picking at a bowl of flowers on the windowsill. She had her back to him and he called her name. She turned but because of the brightness of the window he could not see her face. So he stepped sideways to see her better but the pause before she answered had already told him all he needed to know. If she had been ready to leave she would have come towards him.

'Hello William. How was Edward?'

'He was all right. Beryl –' William moved further to the side to get away from the brightness of the window. Beryl hadn't moved, still touched the flowers which were chrysanthemum heads, browning; petals fell on the sill as she touched them. 'Beryl – all the time on the train when I was coming back I was thinking of you. You were why I was coming back. You've always been why I did everything.' He felt absurd.

'You liked Annette.'

Surely she hadn't been brooding on that all these years. 'But that was nothing, you ...'

'I know. But you liked her. You could have been happy with her. I could have been all right with somebody else. Let's not exaggerate everything.' It was odd to see William in this room, and good to get away from him sometimes.

The flowers were dead. 'A boy was eaten by a shark. The rescuers nearly got there, but not quite. They could only watch.'

William had read about it on the train. Beryl looked at him in that funny way, as though seeing him on the other side of a band of dark. She was probably right to let herself be overcome; there is something grisly about surviving. 'Look,' he said, and went down on his knees; he probably wouldn't have been able to do that if he had thought she was really listening. 'Look Beryl, this is the only world we know we have. You must understand what you've given me. We aren't just together because we're old and it's too late to get anybody else. It's possible we could have been with other people but we're not, we're with each other and there hasn't been a day in the last thirty years when I haven't been glad it was you and not somebody else I can't even imagine. I trust you. Anything I am that's worthwhile is because there's one person in the world I trust. You can't feel badly about a world in which it's possible to do that for another person. We're *not* alone, in the dark. *I'm* not, because of you. But – I don't seem to be able to do the same for you ...'

She looked down at the kneeling figure: the familiar face with the great brows and light brown eyes that seemed to have faded over the years, the whites around the pupils becoming yellower; red ears sticking out from that ridiculous thatch of hair coarse as a broom. He had been so upset when it began to show signs of grey; put blacking on it that left marks on the pillow. He'd given that up after Helen had been to the cottage that time ...

'William, where shall we live?'

'Where we do now Beryl. The same place.'

'Not the country?'

'Not any more. Not if you don't want to.'

'It frightens me ... How was Helen?'

'She wasn't there.'

Beryl nodded, without interest. William's hair was dry, like the chrysanthemum petals and nearly as thick. He should have worn it as the flowers did, radiating out from the centre, it had always looked wrong brushed across. She touched it with stiff fingers, not because of affection but because it was there, like the bowl on the windowsill. She smiled to herself. 'You should have been God.'

William tried to guess what she meant, staring up at her. 'I would like to have made things easier for you ...'

'You brought me your questions,' she said. 'You never answered mine.'

'There *is* no answer.'

'How difficult you made life seem!' Her fingers were still on his hair, curved now to fit his scalp. 'You came to me for encouragement you know.'

William stared down at the worn carpet. He had never felt Beryl needed encouragement. She had never said ... 'Oh Beryl.'

'Mr Henryson!'

William turned, still on his knees. 'It's all right Mrs Turnbull. We're nearly finished.'

'It's not good for us you know!' With set mouth she stared down at him from the door. A female figure with cropped hair stood behind her grinning and nodding. The Matron hesitated, then grasped the woman by the arm. 'Come along dear, it's not time for *Nationwide* yet.' She shut the door brusquely, frowning.

'Why are you kneeling?'

'I wanted to tell you ...'

'I'll be home soon.'

'Yes.' He got up stiffly. He had trained her to be without

him, by failing her. 'Do you want to stay in this room?'

'No. I think I'll go back.'

He could not bear to see the room she shared with three others. 'Shall I take you?'

'No,' said his wife. 'You go now. Goodbye.'

'Beryl!' He heard himself pleading and she drew back. 'Beryl,' he said more firmly, 'that shark, it was awful. It might have been Peter.' He wouldn't tell her he'd invited Peter. 'Sharks are scavengers. There's nothing evil in a shark.'

'Dear shark?' said Beryl. 'Dear William?' She turned at the door and said flatly, 'Feeding all right?'

'I've only just got back.'

She nodded, 'I'll be home soon.' She walked off down the corridor and turned to wave briefly before disappearing into her room.

William stood for a moment at the head of the stairs. Figures shuffled past him, staring.

He walked slowly down and after standing blankly at the matron's door remembered his bag. He considered walking away and leaving it, but he would only have to come back. He waited outside the front door touching a pillar on the porch, looking down at some dusty hydrangeas, greeny-blue, as though their flowers were pretending hopefully they were only leaves.

'You'll be wanting your valise?'

'If you please.'

She made a business of rattling her key-chain, still furious with him. She threw open the door with one hand and as he passed her to collect his case she said: 'It doesn't do you know, upsetting them like that!'

'In what way, upsetting?'

'That one's been upset enough!' She glared at him, her chins shaking.

'You mean my wife's condition is my fault?'

The matron let her silence stand as an answer and then forced a professional smile. 'Ah well we'll be out of here soon enough. Right as rain. Good *day* Mr Henryson.' The smile vanished before the closing door passed it.

In Putney High Street William suddenly put down his

bag and sat on it.

All he had said to Beryl was true, inadequate and irrelevant.

A flight of starlings went overhead, followed by another and another. Though they flew together it was unevenly, as if each starling had reservations about the company it was keeping.

To go blundering in expecting her to be grateful for his kind words! He was a scout-master. Her reaction to life was as valid as his, perhaps more so. Even this sudden glorification of Putney High Street by the evening sun was not an uncommon human experience, it was simply one he chose to pin his faith to.

No. He knew it was the glory that was true. He started to get up and heard his name called. 'Are you feeling poorly?'

Looking up he carefully examined the face of the figure standing over him. 'No. Why?' He thought briefly of giving a lecture on the advantages of sitting for a moment in Putney High Street on a fine evening. How long had he been there? Nowadays he seemed continually to be finding himself looking up at faces in various stages of disapproval, as though he had become a horizontal man in a world of vertical ones.

'I've been looking all over London for you. Your telephone never answered.' The man sounded reproachful. Telephones always made people oddly possessive.

'No,' said William, getting up. He found it difficult and had to press his hand on the pavement, his bag was soft and gave no purchase. 'Nice to see you.'

'How's Beryl?'

'Loopy as ever.'

'Good, good,' the man said, nodding and smiling. His reply, thought William, is at least as sensible as mine. I think I recognise him. But who?

Vertical himself now, he thought he remembered, because of the man's height. Looking down at a pink patch in thinning fair hair he remembered a short, delicate-looking student who had come to see him as part of a group when they lived at – he forgot. He'd not said a word and then suddenly blurted out how much William's books had helped him. That had been nice.

'Derek,' he said, trying it out, keeping the question out of his voice. The man did not disagree so he must be a Derek. Extraordinary!

'I'd like to talk to you. You might be interested in an idea I have. Are you doing anything?'

'No.'

'Shall we have a bite to eat?'

'That'd be nice.' Nicer, anyway, than buying a piece of meat in a white tray and cooking it in the flat till it turned from dead brown to dead grey.

'Let me take that.'

'No of course not.'

'One handle anyway.'

It was extremely awkward because Derek's hand was a foot lower than William's so William took all the weight and the bag at an angle banged his leg. William was breathless by the time they stopped outside a steak house that even from the pavement smelled of old fat.

Inside it smelled of feet, although there appeared to be no one else there. Presumably old feet, thought William, while Derek looked up at a multiplicity of signs: SADDLE ROOM, FISH 'N'FRY, THE NELL GWYNNE. All arrows pointed downwards, away from the evening. 'They do quite a good quick meal here,' Derek said, half-apologetically – perhaps he was the Manager? – and led on down the stairs, deeper into the smell.

It was possible to get used to it, thought William, sniffing, as they sat at their small table in their small booth. It was a cavern filled with small booths, each with its pink-shaded lamp. There was soft music, soft light and they were the only customers. Why did he not have acquaintances who took him to orgies instead of subterranean steak houses? He had wasted his life.

'Have you ever been to an orgy, Derek?'

'Why do you ask? Shall we order?' He did so for them both.

William had forgotten. 'Because I'm interested in people,' he said, feeling cruel.

'You think one might get to know people in that way?'

'I should have thought so, in a sense, yes.'

'But what made you suddenly ask?' Derek was smiling attentively.

William consulted the air; he wondered whether it got into ones' clothes: 'The – atmosphere?'

'Still the old Zen Master. The startling, oblique question. And calling me Derek! That was a good trick!'

William smiled down at his hands enigmatically.

'Penny's a great admirer of your work.'

William looked up in case the man, who was clearly not called Derek, would tell him who Penny was. But he was not hopeful. Something about the steady gaze, the mouth permanently turned up at the corners, proof against snubs, told him a flood of personal reminiscence was about to break over him. Did people become like this because they were lonely or were they lonely because they were like this?

'You're in London permanently now?'

'I am.'

'Country cottages too expensive these days?' His grin became wider and more lifeless, his head was cocked so archly it was almost on a level with the table.

'Yes I'm afraid so.' William's steak arrived. It was rather good.

'You must miss the great god Pan.'

He did remember this fellow. He had not praised one of his books or said it had helped him. He had suddenly said, in a sullen voice, that he thought the whole of William's work was élitist rubbish. It was the only time he had spoken.

'Not at all. He's in London. Always was the god of secret places. No secret places left in the country.'

'In the parks?'

'Oh no. Streets. Man isn't in control there. Thinks he is but isn't. Light. Wind. Pan.'

'The concrete jungle.'

William swallowed. His steak was really very good. He had a picture of buildings like great trees, men slung among their branches in flats and rooms, and between their roots eating in cellars like this one. 'No. The town's not a jungle. Much worse. Only men are greedy.'

'Don't tell me you've become a socialist!'

William was surprised he'd been listening at all. From his expression he had imagined him incapable of taking in any speech longer than a sentence, if it did not concern him and Penny. 'You'd be surprised?'

'I would have thought you'd be the last person to become trendy.'

He must make absolutely certain this person paid for the meal. Now un-Derek, or Penny's bloke, was going on about the Unions, about profit not being a dirty word. 'But first I ought to tell you something about myself,' he ended.

'Perhaps you could begin by telling me your name.'

He did so, evenly, his eyes as usual bleakly resting on William's, waiting for a response. 'We came to visit you, a group of us from college. You spent about an hour with us and then said you were busy.'

'I expect I'd run out of things to say.'

'We'd come a long way.'

'You haven't asked me to supper to tell me how rude I was, I hope?'

'Not at all. You were very nice – as far as it went.'

'Why did you come?'

'Oh the president of the student's union was deep into the nature-kick at the time.'

'And you were not?'

'No. Oddly enough I am now. Penny and I have this cottage in Wales. Miles from anywhere on top of a mountain. We get down there as often as we can and unwind. The kids adore it.'

'So now you can re-read my books with more understanding.' William was enjoying himself.

'I shall look forward to that,' said the man. 'But Penny loves them. She says it's like taking time off from the real world.'

William burst out laughing. 'You really are the most insulting fellow!'

'Why?'

'I thought my books were about the real world you see.'

'Yes of course. I didn't mean that. But they're all about trees and God and stuff. And, hell! We *need* time off from the real world!'

'Do we? I suppose they are about those things,' said William, reflectively. 'You however don't read them.'

'Look. I could have pretended couldn't I? Filled you with guff about my admiration et cetera? Surely someone as established as you are doesn't need all that?'

'It's always nice.'

'Besides I get no time to read in my job. I'm in charge of a books programme for the BBC. I wanted to talk to you about that. But first I ought to tell you what's been happening to Penny and me since we last met. Fill in the background if we're going to work together.'

'I don't remember anyone called ...'

'No we hadn't met then. We married about a year afterwards. She was in her second year, studying the social sciences. Well, a kid came along, that was Adrian, he was a difficult baby in some ways, she started getting her headaches. We decided to have a go in New Zealand. Arthur helped us, he's Penny's uncle. Well not her uncle actually, a friend of her father's ...'

He couldn't be like this with all his customers, he wouldn't hold down his job. He must be a tiger in the control room.

'... got a job as an announcer. God knows what the audience was, a few sheep I shouldn't wonder but it was great experience. And Penny did what social work she could. Then ...'

The other had fallen silent, waiting. 'Your Uncle Alfred sounds like a fairy god-father,' said William.

'Uncle Arthur. Penny's uncle. Yes. The house in Cricklewood was our real saviour.'

'A pleasant spot,' said William vaguely.

'D'you really think so?' the man said, surprised.

'It was interesting to hear all about you both,' William went on quickly. 'Difficult to follow in places, all those names, I'm slow-witted these days I'm afraid. But kind of you to tell me ... Why did you?'

'We don't talk enough to each other. All of us, I mean.'

'No,' said William doubtfully. He had an ache across the top of his spine. This chap was a pain in the neck.

'We all go around in our self-contained boxes, buttoned up. That's what's fascinating about my job. Communication. People, personalities, ideas. Of course you'd have to do a test.'

'I've already done some broadcasting you know. It was rather succ –'

'Amazing how the camera picks up any phoniness.'

'Do you think I'm –'

'Nature's big now. The urban masses lap it up. We need someone of the old school –'

It was William's turn to interrupt, firmly. 'Tell me – do people ever refuse?'

'What?'

'After – you have talked to them, do they ever say no?'

The producer was incredulous. 'They're too vain, or broke, or both! Not that you – I mean – seriously, you interested me when you said there were no secret places left in the country. That's the sort of stuff we want. What did you mean?'

'Farmers now have machines which can get almost anywhere, so they can grub out cover, use land that has been undisturbed since it was first planted.'

His companion looked grave and shook his head. 'Disgraceful.'

'No it's not. The farmers' job is to produce food. So they clear the land. Result: no place for Pan.'

'Or for you.'

'Or me.'

'You should come to Wales. Nothing like owning a few acres. A rootlet. A hundred and thirty actually. Ridiculous, isn't it!'

'You're Welsh?'

'Good Lord no. They're a funny lot round there. Real characters. Completely unspoiled.'

'Who owned your house before you bought it?'

'A small farmer.'

'Where does he live now?'

'In a small bungalow we built him, it was part of the price. It's quite hideous but he's perfectly happy. He didn't even have drains before.'

'The land?'

'Oh it's only hill grazing. The children romp all over it. I work on the house. I've put back the original slate mullions. Sometime last century somebody put in Victorian gothic windows with little leaded panes. Quite pretty but completely inappropriate. We've turned it back into what it must have been, a crude shepherd's bothie, open-plan.'

'You don't think it's a pity, people like us moving to the country?'

'You did.'

'I said people like us.'

'I only *know* about the countryside because people like you wrote about it. And people like me are saving it. We've formed a local amenity society, trying to keep the damned Forestry Commission at bay, having pylons re-routed and so on. You must come and stay.'

'No, I won't do that.'

'But you must, we could talk about the programme.'

'Thank you, no, I'm too old and I'm happy where I am.'

'But you'll do it?'

'The programme? You haven't told me much about it.'

'I thought we'd better get to know each other first. The personal element. It's an open-ended series. If it clicks it could go on for as long as *Desert Island Discs*! A *causerie* about Nature – and people.'

'There's no difference.'

' – I see what you mean, and buildings and events in the countryside. I want someone to structure it, someone with the old values. Nothing too highbrow for Fred and Freda home from work, tired, not wanting to be stretched too far. That's our catchment area. But they want news from where it's at. And that is where it's at, not on the factory floor. Make no mistake. The country can get on without the factory, but not the other way round.'

'Are you sure?'

'Let's find out, that's the fun of it. We could make that the first prog. Or the pilot. The bods upstairs want a pilot but, no bother, they'll buy it, they love the idea. One of them had heard of you by the way.'

'Had he?'

'Yes I was quite surprised. He asked me who I had in mind to front it and I mentioned your name and he said good choice.'

'I am pleased.'

'So you'll do it?'

'It's really very kind of you.'

'That's my boy! It's no good burying your head in the sand.' He put his hand on William's arm. 'I know I seem a brash bastard to you but I'm offering you a whole new audience. Penny'll be delighted.' He paid the bill with a flourish. 'D'you go away much?'

'Er – no. Why?'

'I don't want to lose touch. I've been phoning you for weeks.'

'I just got back from Italy. This afternoon.'

'Really, really Italy, well don't go away again will you there's a good chap. We've got to get this thing off the ground. Here's my number. We'll be in touch. This is going to be exciting.'

William was reluctant to let him go. He had a manner, simultaneously aggressive and placating, which he found comforting.

Outside it was nearly dusk, a warm windless evening, and the producer hailed a cab that was cruising slowly, as if in honour of the peacefulness that had fallen on the town. 'Can I drop you somewhere?'

'No thank you, I'll walk. I don't live far from here.'

'You're a secretive chap.'

'No I'm not.'

'OK, OK!' In the door of the cab the producer waved his palms on either side of his face as though telling a Jewish story. 'No offence. Talent has to be pushed. I've no talent but I can push. Cheers then.'

William loved London on such evenings but there was another reason why he wanted to walk. He had often noticed a church from the top of a bus. It was nearby and he felt the need to visit it. The humour of the producer's presence would fade and leave him exposed. He would like to be in a church when that happened.

A group of young men on the pavement jostled him as he

absent-mindedly tried to make his way between them. He dropped his bag and heard them turning round to laugh as he bent to pick it up.

The church, set behind dusty iron railings, was open, empty and almost completely dark. William settled himself into a pew and allowed some of the unsettlement inside himself to slow down. The meeting with that chap had been confusing as well as amusing. And the meeting with Beryl ... Not much that happened to him did he fully understand, which was true of most people he supposed, and this rather ugly building had presumably been built to contain just such an acknowledgement.

Kneeling, he rested his forehead on the damply sticky pew-back in front of him, smelling the bitter varnish. His eyes shut, the darkness behind them crowded with unidentifiable impressions that had nothing to say for themselves yet, so he opened them and regarded the dark silhouette of an angel that presided over the church from behind the altar.

It was quiet, except for the creakings and sighings of furniture common to such places. Possibly there was an old lady in the dark somewhere at the back, or a tramp stretched out asleep.

The angel, what William could see of it, looked well done. Life-size, possibly of some plaster substance but more likely of gilded wood. Its wings were formalised, not pinions sprouting uncomfortably from shoulder-blades but bars and rods, light rays, so the angel stood inside a fence of solidified light.

William believed in angels, like Petrarch. We reach a blankness – and beyond the blankness we hear the rustle of wings. The silence of the wooden angel affected William like the silence of a tree. The figure was not growing but it was not dead either, because it represented an aspiration. In the angel he saluted his brother, the maker of the angel. We only have humble means to work with: in this case plaster, wood, golden paint. He prayed for the soft furl of wings round the boys who had bumped him outside, round Beryl. He could feel the soft underdown, it was a time and a place to yield, let go, lose purpose, remorse, relax the strain of standing upright on the spinning world. It was not a desire for death or to be on all fours, not at all. He knew he would be refreshed if he could let himself lapse, let himself loose ... Startled, he heard the rustle of wings.

A clergyman stood at his side fiddling with a loose umbrella. He remembered he had heard a flurry of rain a few moments earlier.

'Just sheltering?' said the clergyman, smiling inquisitively behind steel-rimmed glasses.

'No,' said William, forcing himself to smile too.

'You've come to see the pictures.'

'No.'

'Perhaps you would care to look at them? We embarked on the work six months ago and it is progressing well. Though expensive.' He looked sideways at William as though assessing his possible contribution. The angel retreated back into the darkness. William rose and followed the small black figure to the side of the church where he switched on a light, revealing buckets and ladders and workmen's paraphernalia. In the process of being scraped clean on the side walls was a series of ceramic pictures of the life of Jesus done in thin colours. They reminded William of the food hall in Harrods.

'Rather fine, don't you think?'

'Better than whitewash,' said William politely. 'I like your angel.'

'Which one?'

William indicated but the vicar did not turn; he pointed to another in front of them, which simpered. 'This one's rather fine. I don't believe I've seen you before, are you a local resident? Perhaps you attend St James's?'

'No,' said William. He had had enough of questions, and of the loneliness of others. He had got what he came in for.

Afterwards he was haunted, as he always was by his evasions. The small black figure with the flapping umbrella had so clearly wanted conversation and he had refused him. No wonder the angel had retreated. Anyway, he should have told him that he'd come into the church not to shelter, or look at the wall-tiles, but to pray.

People and Weather

It would be the same with the television programme. He would be quirky but obedient, concealing his real thought. The series would end, or his participation in it, with friendliness and puzzlement.

He stood at the window sipping cocoa, wishing it was whisky, looking down at the traffic. There was a dirty plate and a glass on his work-table; he had left in a hurry to catch his train for Italy. There was work on the table, hack-work he doubted he had the heart to finish. It would have been better in the country, the loneliness he felt, but London was better for Beryl and he had to be near the source of odd jobs. Besides, the rate of ripping and tearing in the country had begun to make him gibber.

On the whole he preferred vicars in dark churches, watchful as mice, broadcasting men with their heads on one side like thrushes listening for worms, and lonely, violent boys.

In the programme he would try not to give the game away, that there was really not much left to celebrate. 'As long as *Desert Island Discs* ...' The telephone was dusty. He dictated another cable. CAN HELP PAY RETURN FARES LOVE DADDY. He hoped the producer would not let him down. He needed his family. He needed to be near people who reached his heart.

At the back of the house was a fire-escape and he climbed down it into the little garden. The sky was orange with reflected street lights and the tall trees were black against it. Through a gate in the garden wall he let himself into the park, which was a semi-private one, belonging to the houses built around it. This was Beryl's concession to his love for trees and grass – she had found this place. As he opened the small green-painted door with its corroded latch, tugging at it because it was warped, it knocked a small round object that lay against it which made a bristly grating sound. He bent down to see what it was; a hedgehog. Among mouldy leaves they both crouched together in the continuous sighing of the traffic on the other side of the houses. William kept still and after a while the hedgehog put out its small intelligent face, its little pig-like eye glinting in a shaft of light. He gave it a small shove and it scuttled to cover, not very fast, its claws making a scratching noise on the greasy paving of the path. William stood up, glad it had been alive. If Beryl had been there it would have been dead.

Once he had invited her to look in a nest before he had looked in it himself. The five nestlings had all had their heads recently bitten off. He had looked in thousands of nests and never seen such a thing.

In the park he stood below a fine copper beech. He had tried not to let Beryl know how little trees in towns impressed him. They were there on sufferance, abiding the whim of their masters like animals in zoos. He saluted the beech with fellow-feeling. He wondered how Peter saw the future, he might be able to ask him. But knowing Peter he would just puff on his pipe and smile. Perhaps by now he had developed opinions about such matters. William found himself hoping he had not.

He walked the dark path that bordered the edge of the park overhung with holly and laburnum and tangled hawthorn, half-listening to an odd mechanical noise he could not place, different from the hum of the traffic; past toys abandoned for the night at the park-doors of the houses, slowly deflating plastic footballs, dented tricycles; past the constantly replenished pile of rubbish thrown over the park wall by the council tenants who were not allowed inside. When he had first come here he had found some children hanging over the wall and had invited them in. They tore up the flowers and all the smaller shrubs they had time to reach; they burned down the gardener's shed, which contained the communal motor-mower.

That was what he had been hearing, or presumably its replacement. He turned a corner and looked out of darkness onto a patch of sward. Elizabeth their neighbour, bent almost horizontal over the handles, was mowing in the dark, rapt, speeding along in straight lines, swinging it round at the end of each line so fast her chin almost touched the motor. Elizabeth, protector of stranded swifts – she had worn one on her shoulder like a brooch all through a winter, trying to keep it alive till the warm weather came. She failed. Protector and cherisher of each plant and shrub and tree in the park, friend of the children who climbed in also, feeder of hedgehogs, rescuer of stray cats and stray people, sometimes almost hysterical in the degree of her involvement and her lone determination to help.

That is what he would do. He would buy some whisky in the pub if it was still open and invite Elizabeth for a drink. He liked talking to Elizabeth, she was brave. He hesitated to interrupt her. Up and down she went as he stood watching, her hair streaked across her forehead with sweat, fiercely cherishing her small patch of green, endlessly mowing the communal grass in the dark, or in London what passes for dark.

Endpiece

The children were annoying, it was difficult to find a place to work and they touched his papers. Irritably, helplessly he found on waking each morning they were the people he wanted to see.

He searched Pete's bland face for the child he had loved, sometimes successfully. Peter was cool, life did not seem to bother him much; William thought he remembered he had always been like that. It was difficult to find common subjects and any direct question put to Peter about his life was apt to be answered by his wife Martha. She was fond of the first person plural: 'Oh we love that, don't we Sam' – she always called him Sam and William found himself doing so too, as though there were now two people, young Peter and grown-up bespectacled Sam. Besides, it seemed discourteous to call him Peter when his wife insisted on another name. When he was answered for, Sam would smile, making no reply, as though slightly deaf. William wondered if he was indeed deaf and played small tricks on him like offering him more food in a quiet voice (he was very greedy) but could never quite make up his mind. In order to escape Martha he took him out to pubs where they drank Young's bitter, but William recognised that her Sam showed no eagerness to be separated from the talkative Martha and supposed he ought to be grateful that his son was so contentedly married.

Peter, although he did not say so, rather disliked the beer which gave him a slight headache. He had doubts about its hygiene too, it tasted to him as though it had already been used for something else, but he put up with it because it seemed to give his father pleasure, and all the people they talked with agreed .it was the best beer in London. He missed his home, which was so much more comfortable, and his friends who never went in for the endless questionings and probings of old tired England and, yes, of his old tired father. For he was slower now and sometimes in repose his face had a melancholy drained look, but his eye, always turned on Peter so smilingly, still had behind it the watching and judging expression that Peter remembered from his boyhood. In those days he had tried to live up to the simplicities it demanded of him. Now it made him restless and uneasy, his friends at home did not look at each other like that; we are all, he thought, too self-involved maybe but we get on with it and make life as much fun as we can, not all this testing and scratching, it's creepy. But from his father he didn't really mind it. Somewhere he had a big reservoir of affection for the old boy though he realized, looking round the poky flat, that one day he was going to have to take him on financially.

His mother he kept clear of. Her quickness, unlike his father's, had always made him feel stupid. He was not surprised it had ended in over-strained nerves. But she kept the lid on them fairly well now; she had always been tough.

William, despite the garden and the park, finding the six of them too much at close quarters and seeing Beryl's eye beginning to rest, more and more glitteringly, on the ineffable Martha, took them all to the seaside. This was an unusual dead-lift for him, he usually left such daring initiatives to others, but he thought circumstances required it.

They sat on a pebbly beach behind breakwaters out of the wind, Martha talking, Sam pottering in bermuda shorts and sneakers looking for prawns among the rocks, Beryl, slightly apart, turning the pages of a book at regular intervals, and the children sprawling all over William.

He liked that; he liked the pliancy of their bones and found them more entertaining than his adult companions. It was possible to tell precisely what they were feeling and they were easier to amuse. They were a good excuse to get away from Martha, and they clambered into cliff caves led by a panting William. He liked talking to them and listening to them, they were thirsty and delicate like flowers, were part of the movement of nature in which now he put the whole of his trust. Not 'Mother Nature' which was a dangerous idea, leading us to expect help and find only ruthlessness, but sister nature, our equal, all under God subject to the same laws and with the same strange power of recurrence. Huddled in caves with the children he felt part of them and part of the rocks and the sky and the grey lapping sea. It was the world of poetic truth, not grown-up truth, and watching the adults on the shingle he saw Beryl lay aside her book and turn deliberately to Martha. He hoped the looked-for confrontation was not going to take place. Peter was a burly speck, far out with his net among the green and brown rocks.

On a cold afternoon they went to the fun-fair, Beryl disapproving. She followed behind, watching William, who had a child on either side of him, holding their hands. Sam as usual had wandered off; mercifully, for once, taking Martha with him. William bent first to one side, then to the other, as he tried to hear the children above the appalling din of the fairground. Beryl licked an ice-cream, trying to look as much a part of the party as she could bear to. She hated it, the noise, the cruelty – there was even a peep-show of a girl in a cage with rats – and she saw the white puzzled faces of the children as they stared up at the stooping William, both of the boys stunned by the row and the bustle.

She hated his sentimentality. He was taking false nourishment from their youngness. He almost shunned her company, though she tried not to be too depressing. She did not blame him. He had always been a survivor. But it was false, and a betrayal. Life was mean and cruel and if only we would stop pretending it was otherwise! If we could admit the truth and face it then life could begin afresh, clear, pared, possible. But we shrank, evaded, like William. Instead of looking at the bleakness of our destination he turned his back on it, leaving her to walk on alone, while he stayed behind and sucked on little pleasures.

They stood by a shooting gallery. A row of pocked metal figures moved slowly along a line and disappeared, reappearing at the other side. Whether they were shot down or not they all vanished in the end on the inexorable slow-moving belt.

She could not bear it, she made an exclamation and put her hands over her face. 'What's the matter granny, what's the matter granny?' squeaked Gregory who had already been frightened enough by the place. William turned to see what Beryl had been looking at and quickly took her by the elbow.

He was always quick, he always understood, she wondered what bromide he was going to offer her now.

The children were now wailing and punching each other, pebble-eyed. William, hanging on to them, stared at the slow procession of figures which had not contact with each other, just things to be shot at and then on to disappearance, in the shape of men. Do I have any connection with Peter, did I with my father, do these two lightless brats with theirs? Is there any connectedness anywhere? And am I thinking my own thoughts or Beryl's?

William found a small open-air café outside the fairground and they sat there, the children running about under the tables, filthy, annoying the one-armed proprietor. Beryl dabbed at spilt lemonade on the table with her handkerchief. 'Well' she said, looking at him, 'what do we do now?' He hated her.

His eyes followed the children. They had found an old-fashioned drinking fountain, operated by pushing a brass button. Because of some maladjustment the water spouted up from the centre of the basin far too high, sousing the face of the drinker. The boys were trying it out, screaming with laughter; the people at the café watched them blankly, or with disapproval. William left Beryl and went over to try the fountain. It was indeed startling, impossible to judge how high the water would come so that your face was deliciously drenched by a jet of cold water. He began to invent, as the children had been inventing, different ways of being surprised by the water. Then Hugh, playing Oliver Hardy to Gregory's Stan did an excellent imitation of Oliver's long-suffering slow-burn, turning his dripping face to the ever incompetent Stan.

It was all that mattered: responsiveness to what was.

William felt he was learning again, the children reminding him. Invention, responsiveness, play. It was all right, the day and the world was saved. The children were clean again, so was he, Beryl was wrong. Poor Beryl.

The three of them went over to where she sat, William taking her hand, squeezing it, hoping for some small pressure back. She smiled, tautly rejecting his solace to the wounded. She was very determined. William felt his nerves drawn tight by her silence. The children were inventing something again, had found an echoing drain to shout down. He was determined too.

Back in London William and Peter got on better. He found again the way to make Peter laugh, which was the same as it had been in the past when it was their great bond. He had to be unfatherly, undignified, and Peter responded at once, relaxing. William had never had any idea how formidable, and formidably demanding, he was. All he had to do was to play the buffoon that most of the time he felt himself to be anyway and Peter and he got on famously, as equals.

When they left it was with the promise to return next year which, though expensive, William was determined should happen. He did not want to miss the growing-up of the children and blessed Peter for marrying late and thus bringing him this pleasure when he was at a stage to notice it.

Money was coming in. The programme was popular and was becoming more and more ridiculous. William found himself reciting the praises of May in Gloucestershire, harvest-time in Orkney, the rural Christmas, which became more and more encomiastic as the meaning, even the existence, of these things receded. He ransacked his old notebooks for phrases, astonished to see how well, once, he had written. He had no sense of self-betrayal, or only a mild one; on the whole he was amused, and he was certainly not betraying the things he talked about because if these had any reality it was beyond the power of his words.

As with Sam he had no idea of the pressures he put on Beryl. He seemed to wander through the world like a minor god – *very* minor, she reminded herself grimly. It was as though, feeling himself a part of creation, he also considered himself, comfortably, a part-creator; creator and created being for him constituents of the same process, complementary, co-existent. Whereas to Beryl we were a part of nothing, or of "nothingness", if she wished to sound portentous to herself. His sudden asperities and exasperations frightened her because they only added to the burden of proof: after so many years even she, even William, could not understand each other. She had no wish to dampen him, he should have known that, but she could not laugh at his little jokes, respond to his chat. It was not as if he had any respect for his own beliefs either: he did a weekly parody of himself on the television which it was understood between them she never watched. Once was enough.

For his part William couldn't function properly without things and people to love. He found enough in the day to keep him going, usually: a shape, a colour, even in London. Or more especially in London because it seemed to fall like an unsolicited blessing.

He thought Beryl might have cheered up a bit if she loved something. Him for instance. It was a gloomy look out, really, if there was nothing left of what had been between them.

But he shrank from confronting her. Like great slag-heaps their days and years together stood in piles all round them, obstructing the view. Impossible to sift through that and find the pieces that fermented, poisoning the air. Anyway, the air wasn't poisoned. Beryl was just going through a bad patch. She needed a big hug. Sometimes he tried to give her one and she was like a piece of wood. At other times, true, she approached him; but at the wrong times. Hurt, chilled, he could not respond either. It was all very tiring.

A letter arrived from Edward. Months before he had fallen out of a cherry tree and broken his leg. The leg had been set badly, he had had an operation for re-setting and now he had septicemia in hospital.

'Did they improve medical care in the quattrocento? They certainly haven't moved on since, not here. We're left alone all day, we've plastic bags by our beds filled with old crusts we gnaw on. The ward's an old monks' dormitory I think. Regards to Beryl by the way. Sorry about our conversations. You're not really a prig yourself but you're a powerful cause of priggishness in others. We all struggle to survive here, me included. I might have considered jumping off the world but I've no intention of being pushed.

High up opposite my bed is a fresco. By Pinturrichio, I'm told. They daren't clean it in case they spoil it. The dirt got into my leg. Pinturrichio's Revenge.

I'll limp because of Mother Church. Your God and your Grace have got into my leg. And your Art.

I hear from Emma things are bad in England. She's working in a coffee bar to be near her Dad. She really loves that guy.

There's one chap who's looking *out* of the picture, over his shoulder, as though he's just seen something fascinating like you. I feel I could talk him out of it. Maybe. I watch him as the light shifts. He seems very certain, in one world, looking back into another, into mine.

I am kept going by a new healthy vein of misogyny. I have come to detest the female principle. Women are the most frightful bores, without exception. Emotionally self-indulgent, intellectually lazy and narrow as drains. As long as they are women. We all grow whiskers in the end.

I have a new picture of myself, gaunt, yellow and alone, like a retired officer in Conan Doyle. Limping around the farm doing what I can to control rebellious nature. Losing, but fighting. Keeping a patch almost alive. Not a bad way to see out the collapse of the old order. Then – wrap me up in my tarpaulin jacket.

This is drab stuff. See you at the pearly gates, if not before. Christianity vulgarizes death. Love Edward.'

William handed the letter to Beryl who read it quickly and threw it on the table.

'Absurd, about that picture,' said William.

'He's trying to make a symbol out of it.'

'No – I mean – why don't they move it? They're frightfully good at that, the Florentines.'

'He's trying to make a symbol out of himself.'

People and Weather

'You don't like what he said about women?'

'It's the only thing he says which isn't ridiculously self-conscious!'

William was surprised at her vehemence and wondered for the first time if she could possibly be jealous of his relations with Edward. He had never imagined she could be jealous about anything to do with him, she was so self-sufficient and critical. But she had no equivalent friend herself.

William in fact never got back to Italy, there was never enough money and Beryl could not be left. She was much better, her swings of mood became less extreme. Instead she became more violent in speech and movement, jerky, as though fighting against something, or alongside something, William was never sure which. She seemed to need him with her, or at least she needed somebody with her and he was there.

He took to kneeling by their bed at night-time, before getting into it. This embarrassed and annoyed her, at least he presumed it did because it was embarrassing and annoying, but he did not mind because he was getting old now and it was time to please himself in such ways.

He knelt at other times too, she sometimes surprised him doing it. He found the kneeling easy, he felt impelled to and attached no great significance to the impulse. It certainly represented no advance in holiness. He simply enjoyed it.

What he did while kneeling he could not have described as prayer although presumably that is what it was. He felt a pressure and confusion in his head which lifted when he adopted that position and closed his eyes. Inside the dark he searched for what he needed.

Sometimes it came as a light, settling on his eyeballs and thence slowly down inside him. At other times he could recreate the sensations of his accident when, he had always presumed, he had hung between life and death. Then in a series of flashes – again the experience was one of light – he was conscious of some part of his being leaping from point to point, surely, surprisingly, going from flash to flash like a spark along a fuse except that there was darkness between the flashes, but easily traversed. Then he seemed to arrive at a point ... where he existed as himself and yet did not exist, at least not in terms of ordinary consciousness. He existed purely, and so did all other things, animate and inanimate, and there was a great peace, as far from rest or sleep as could be imagined, filled with energy and clarity, like the sudden perception of a solution to a problem. Whether he was praying or not, or talking to God or not, he had no idea, but he nearly always stood up refreshed and, for a while afterwards, self-forgetful. And in the midst of it he was sometimes conscious of saying, like a gasp forced out of him, 'God forgive me, God help me, God help us all.' Well, He did. So when occasion demanded William knelt.

In books and journals of the time he noticed it had become a commonplace to contrast a presupposition of what should be with the horror of what was and this opposition was set up in a context of bitterness and anger. William could never understand the grounds for this presupposition of the good that *should* be. On the contrary, it had always struck him that on the whole the world was infinitely better than it *could* be. The motion of the air that made tree branches flash lighter and darker – the air could have been still, the light constant. Birds could have been dumb – there could have been no birds or they could all have been the same size and colour, as in nightmares.

As the boys grew older they sometimes came by themselves and their annual visit fascinated him as well as enchanting him. Their freshness and delight in life – no day could begin too soon for them, or end too late – was normal, but it could have been normal for children to be born sullen. Sometimes of course these children became so, and spiteful. But they could have been like that all the time. The tortures and horrors of the world were in these children's hearts and in his own. But such horrors were not everywhere, and even where they were they were not all the time. They could have been.

It was thus he arrived at his idea of a merciful God. Merciful because however wicked men were it was possible for them to be so entirely and for the greater part of their time they were not. William understood God to be surprised at good, rather than enraged at bad. He had His own ideas of what constituted perfection. Although whenever William thought of God in terms of personality, which he tried not to do, he was conscious of a God who turned his face away in weariness, as sometimes William did himself.

When William thought of the mild enduring patience of most lives he believed that the majority of people felt roughly as he did: certainly most of the people he knew behaved as though life were admirable though they never said so, possibly from fear of being thought soft-headed.

So he was trying to set it all down in a book simply, but it was very difficult because we are all eager for a too easy comfort and ordinary words are slippery. However, he secretly believed, such is the vanity of authors, that he was not writing a book out of the past but the book of the future. For the present mood of petulance at reality was an inadequate response to our brief passage on earth and people would soon notice that. His heart sagged often, but he kept at it.

In front of the boys he was a simplified version of himself. He could afford to be, they did not contradict. Beryl saw he had found his perfect audience and was contented.

When they came alone the physical care of the boys fell upon her, grannie, it was she who had to attend to their appetites and tidy up after them and was therefore the daily witness of their carelessness and greed. She resented having to do these things, resented the assumption that it was inevitably her job to do them. She did not resent the boys, who had for her the charm of healthy animals, but she intensely disliked the animal nature of her own role which, in the organism the four of them made, was roughly analogous to that of the stomach: ingestion, digestion and the elimination of waste products. Whereas William, in the organism, represented the mind. What about her mind, and the minds of all stomach-women?

She could see no solution to the problem; greater help in stomach-duties was a help but not a solution. William did, these days, help much more than he used to. If she had not been there the three males would have muddled along quite happily. That knowledge did not help at all. What was she, what were all women, *for*?

She had a soul all right, just as much as William had, lumbering up from his knees to clamber into their bed. She respected William's simplicities but to her they were elephantine.

She knew of course that he had his own black moments also but they could never share them; whenever they tried they ended up shouting at each other, as though to drown the noise of their own shared fears.

She would not break; she had nearly done so, but she would not now. By any standard, it seemed to her, to do so would be a failure. But the temptation to give way was enormous, to be borne away on a tide of feeling, to be swept into the charge of others. The glass told her that the struggle to resist had made her face harder than she felt and thin-mouthed. William helped her. In his odd way he was kindly. Possibly he partially understood. He was not to blame, nor was she, if that was not enough. It would have been terrible, because too small a thing, if it had been.

What she did not know was how much she helped him. She ran the practical side of their lives more single-handedly than he was sometimes prepared to admit, but above all she constantly surprised him. There were large areas in which he operated on the basis of ideas he had adopted in his youth because they seemed to him roughly to fit the case. But she, staring out at the world from her deep sockets, was more aware of motion than static William, she felt the shifts of emphasis and changes of need more acutely than he and was, though she never would have thought it of herself, more a part of her own times. Thus she was occasionally able to bring him up short, whether roughly or gently, and he would pause, grateful to her, and decide she was right and he had become wrong. When their friends came she kept the conversation sharp and William noticed they often preferred to listen to her than to him. He did not mind, he preferred listening to her himself. The friends usually left rather excited, though there had been occasions when somebody they did not know too well, argued at by her, floored, had become shrill in self-defence. She did not seem to notice this.

She had intellect, courage and hardly any imagination. William would have had her no other way. Though sometimes he could have wished, for his own comfort, that her energy was less spasmodic.

About this time in another part of England a handsome woman with heavy eyebrows pulled up her car on a narrow treeless road and got out to stretch her legs. She was not quite sure why she had stopped but she obediently stretched and supposed it was because of the pony she had seen on the skyline. She was thinking of buying ponies for the children, her husband came of horsy stock and she'd become interested herself. She looked round, memorising the place, she would be passing along there fairly often when the children went to their boarding schools, and it seemed vaguely familiar. Then she remembered. There were fewer trees and hedges but that was the same now all over England. She turned her head and there was the path leading across the field; it was tarmac now and led to a newish housing estate with most of the houses still for sale, though the advertisements looked pretty old. William's house had gone and she could see, climbing the rungs of a metal gate, that the spring behind it where he used to dabble had also gone, and the hedge above it; now there was a large square of concrete with ventilating pipes sticking out of it; presumably the septic tank for the estate. Well, people had to live somewhere, though it did not seem as though many lived here. Probably it was a speculation, left over from the time when such things were profitable. Toby had nearly burned his fingers in just such a venture but fortunately he had not been too heavily involved. Their own part of the country was still more or less uninvaded, though it was a constant battle on the part of themselves and their friends to keep it so.

It was years since she had heard anything of William, the last of the old-school nature lovers. But even then he had been fighting a losing battle. She had not much affection for the girl who had walked down that track when it was different. She had worn a red hat and mac, and had been puzzled by the slight withdrawal she had noticed in

Edward, imagining she could cope. She had heard he had hurt his leg. She imagined him limping round the farm, otherwise unchanged. He could never change. Toby regretted the farm, said they could have used it as a holiday place. But the children would have it eventually. Or Edward might give it up. Toby was good with the children. Edward had never asked to see them.

She turned back to the car firmly. The school she was going to was rather a frightening place, rather drab, but it still tried to turn out the type that had served England well enough in the past. What was wrong with that? Edward would never agree. He never tried. Preferred to watch things getting into a mess.

Using the driver's seat as a step she took a last distant look at the pony which was scratching its neck on the gate. It was a scrawny beast and pretty old but looked docile. She let in the clutch and prepared herself for the final interview with the headmaster. She would miss the children. He was the same kind of man as Toby, an old school friend of his, but not so nice. He frightened her a little.

The next summer the splendidly re-constituted machine that was William's body began seriously to slow down. He began to shuffle. It was the changed sound of his step that most frightened Beryl. He had used his second chance so oddly, so undynamically, as though he had all the time in the world. Instead of moving forward he had gone back, to an age of faith, just when the last remnants of the faith were disappearing. Intolerant, easily exasperated, as forthright in expression as he had ever been, as exclusive in his friendships, yet he had managed to suggest, at the same time, a gradual increase in gentleness and humour. His was, Beryl supposed, from that point of view a successful life. He had become a sort of monk. All very well, but where were his fellow monks? And where did that leave her?

The boys were over at the time and of course they noticed the change in him. They were thrown more together, it was not so much fun, but William gave them what time his energy allowed him and they were extraordinarily understanding. They appeared to accept the process as natural – had probably always thought William was as old as God anyway – but Beryl caught Gregory looking at William with a scared expression. Hugh was as boisterous and cheerful as ever.

One morning they were hanging about on the landing outside their grandparents' bedroom door. They should have been outside on their bicycles but Beryl had found them difficult to move. There was some vague plan for an expedition with William. She doubted whether he'd be able to make it, he'd had a disturbed night and had not yet appeared, but the boys seemed unwilling to give up the chance. They certainly doted on the old boy!

Gregory, greatly daring and feeling guilty because he liked to respect his grandparents' privacy, glanced through the slightly open door. It was bright inside the room after the darkness of the landing and his grandfather was kneeling by his bed in his pyjamas, his head on the orange bedcover. They had caught him like that once or twice before and, slightly embarassed, they had tried to tiptoe away, always to be called back by William, levering himself to his feet. Gregory was about to move away now, feeling Hugh peering over his shoulder – he *would*! – when something stopped him and he knocked gently on the door. There was no reply and still not quite knowing why he did so he gently pushed it open and stepped in. There was something about the stillness of his grandfather at the side of the bed. He turned and ran from the room, bumping right into Hugh, pushing him aside. 'Grannie! Grannie!'

She was in the kitchen, a cigarette in her mouth, doing *The Times* crossword.

'Grannie? It's William. I think he's been taken ill or something!'

Beryl, looking at the white faces of the boys, felt her stomach clench. 'All right, keep calm. Why don't you leave the old chap alone? I'll go up. You stay here.'

She climbed the stairs quickly, the boys following her, and as soon as she saw William everything was clearer to her than it had been for a long time. He would have to be moved, she could not do it herself, she must ask the boys to help her. No, she could not do that. She turned and shoo'd them out of the room. 'I'll see you in a minute. Go downstairs, there's good boys, and stay there.' Frightened, they turned and did as they were told.

She looked at William with an odd mixture of feelings. She went over and touched his still thick hair. He could not be left like that. How like him to be found in that awkward, annoying position! She went to the window, gathering herself. But she did not need gathering. She was conscious of a succession of states: there was one she half-consciously kept for later, for when she understood, but above it there lay relief, a burden had been lifted. Then came thoughts about money. Things had been becoming difficult. William had escaped at the right time.

She felt no guilt at such thoughts, far from it, William would have understood; she felt clear-headed, commonsensical; and from below it all she felt rising up a greater, simpler warmth than had been available to her since she was a child. It was as though her temperament and William's had joined, supplementing each other without conflict. Hers was not taken over by his, not at all, she was her own woman, stronger by her knowledge of William. There was no argument now. No one should criticize him while she lived.

She went downstairs to telephone the doctor. She heard Gregory quietly close himself into his room. Hugh stood by her helplessly while she looked up the number. She put her arm round him and gave him a peck on the cheek. 'I'll talk to you both in a minute. We'll all have a talk.' She must help the boys, especially Gregory, whose desolation she could feel, wafting from behind his shut door. She would be able to. It was odd she should feel so charged with life. And yet, not odd at all. They had been on a journey together and now he had left her to go on another part of the journey by himself. Or so he would have put it … She was smiling as she dialled. It was as though he were helping her. Well — possibly he was. It was undeniable she felt helped. Now, it was easy, she could let him.